Peter Hussey is a previously published author and a retired radiological control technologist, now living with his elder sister, Marty, in Augusta, Georgia. When he isn't treading water down at the local YMCA, Peter spends his time dreaming up plausible science-fiction plots laced with intriguing characters. As an avid non-fiction science reader, he tries to incorporate real startling phenomena in his stories whenever possible, believing that it makes the story more relevant, thought provoking, and enjoyable.

In addition to Marty, Peter has another great sister and four fine brothers, comprising a close-knit family.

To my mother, Anne. Thank you for making reading so much fun for a little dyslexic boy.

To my father, Richard. Thank you for introducing me to the joys of adventure fiction novels and introducing me to our neighborhood public library.

To Dr. C. Richard Dawkins who, more than anyone, makes the pursuit of science grand and the goals of atheism noble.

Peter Hussey

Astro-Avian Apocalypse

For Johnny,
Thanks for all the support! I sure hope you enjoy! Love Ya, Pete

Austin Macauley Publishers™
London · Cambridge · New York · Sharjah

Ordering Information:
Quantity sales: special discounts are available on quantity purchases by corporations, associations, and others. For details, contact the publisher at the address below.

Publisher's Cataloging-in-Publication data
Hussey, Peter
Astro-Avian Apocalypse

ISBN 9781641829533 (Paperback)
ISBN 9781641829540 (Hardback)
ISBN 9781645366508 (ePub e-book)

Library of congress Control number: 2019907905

The main category of the book — Fiction / Science Fiction / General

www.austinmacauley.com/us

First Published (2019)
Austin Macauley Publishers LLC
40 Wall Street, 28th Floor
New York, NY 10005
USA
mail-usa@austinmacauley.com
+1 (646) 5125767

I would like to acknowledge the help of the production and marketing teams of the publishers for their patience and professionalism in publishing this book.

I would also like to thank my brother, Joe, for his thorough review of my manuscript and unwavering enthusiasm. Thanks to all of my great family and thanks to all the great teachers and coaches I've had throughout the years.

Lastly, I wish to thank my dear friend, Ron Levine, for his immense patience and masterful technical support as he guided me through all the confusing complexities of my personal computer.

I. The View from Afar, Very Afar

At a pre-programmed destination some 150 million miles from Earth, hiding within the asteroid belt between the planets Mars and Jupiter, Klaarongah gently flipped a view enhancer switch. She stared in awe at the blue and white jewel of a planet which filled the entire upper-deck viewing screen. She startled suddenly, as her concentration was interrupted, then rapidly flutter-clapped her monstrous beak in mock disgust in response at having just been goosed by her loving companion and fellow stellar-pilot, Krawwgh. He had waddled up behind her to marvel at the view while also copping a feel. Only a few hours earlier, the pair of alien astronauts—two of their world's best candidates for this first-ever, manned interstellar mission—and the only living things onboard their colossal vessel, awoke from six-decade-long induced comas, in order to review current events on their home world, Kaarp, as well as to be brought up to date on their mission, planet Earth.

They were only early teenagers when they were selected from among their elite peers to board the fateful mission to this beautiful blue water-world that circled its lone yellow star a 12 light-years' distance from their home world, Kaarp. Back then, various Kaarpian scientists from numerous fields of study had already been analyzing Earth for several years. Not long after some of the first powerful radio transmissions began radiating from its surface. This formed a gigantic signal bubble that expanded outward at the speed of light. By the mid-1950s back on Earth, these aliens were just beginning to detect human presence and tuned in on the emitted signals from World War II. Upon reception of these first broadcasts, they immediately aimed all of their electro-magnetic radiation analyzers in the direction of Earth, to learn whatever they could about their new, noisy, neighbors.

The krrugh of planet Kaarp were truly thrilled to learn of another intelligent species existence, and on a world located within their own stellar backyard. As they learned more about humans, however, they became shocked and disgusted at all the war, poverty, pollution, and extinction humanity was causing on their precious world. Having already sent many planetary probes out to other possible life-supporting worlds within their stellar neighborhood, three things were becoming abundantly clear to the scientist of Kaarp. One: multi-cellular life-forms were pretty rare in this section of the Milky Way Galaxy, two: planet Earth was an incredible exception but harbored a particularly menacing species, and three: upon this world alone existed a creature that offered a glimmer of hope for their own doomed future.

After much deliberation and planning, a manned mission was formed to send two of their very best youth on the incredibly long and perilous journey to eradicate the disastrous species of apes, known as humans, and then, remediate and reset the planet's ecological balances. Lastly, the two intrepid mission specialist were to locate, protect, and then attempt mating, with the largest and sturdiest species of the flightless birds on Earth, the mighty ostrich. This was a desperate plan to save as many features of their own doomed species and culture as possible, by creating a sophisticated hybrid with the physically well-developed, but intellectually primitive, birds. By the time the two brave explorers reached Earth and completed their mission, all the krrugh back on Kaarp would be dead or very old and dying, and any news of success or failure they sent back would likely never be received.

Klaarongah and Krawwgh learned all this and so much more, as they underwent incredibly rigorous and mentally challenging training in preparation for the mission. In addition to the exhausting and arcane things they had to learn and endure, they had to come to grips with the heart-wrenching realization that, once the journey began, they would never again see any of their family and friends as theirs was a one-way ticket only, in a last ditch effort to save one world, while rekindling their own race. Klaarongah and Krawwgh knew what an honor it was for them to be selected for the mission, and just how important their successful completion of all the mission objectives would be. Together, they represented the most fervent hopes of their world. Thus, for a few days after their training, and before the final mission preparations, and then the induced comas, Klaarongah and Krawwgh engaged in a series of honorary and ceremonial feasts with their mission advisers and governing officials, while also setting aside as much personal time as possible, to cherish their families and friends. They withheld nothing, as they expressed all their love and joy at being among their loved ones, but also, the profound sorrow of knowing they would soon be physically separated, forever. This was the frightening and unavoidable cost imposed by such a vast universe. Within the social customs and norms of their emotionally open and engaged society, they partied excessively and participated in many orgies in an attempt to express and experience as much love, lust, and closeness as possible. Once they began their journey, all they'd have was one another, among the creatures of a new world.

In addition to the honesty and engagement with one another, the other part of the social cement that glued all krrugh together in their all-inclusive monoculture was the level of attention and effort required to communicate. Having evolved from large beaked raptors—giant predatory birds that chomped, crushed, and swallowed whole chunks of prey meat—they did not possess the necessary genetic material with which to eventually evolve highly articulated and agile palates and tongues, required to make the many varied and controlled sounds for a spoken language. Instead, these creatures said it with DANCE! Utilizing their extraordinary visual acuity, computer-like memory, and incredible physical coordination, all krrugh memorized and tirelessly rehearsed demonstrated movements, to learn how to communicate. Starting thousands of centuries ago, as soon as a hatchling was born into its dangerous world along the salt marshes, its survival strongly depended on its abilities to mimic and learn from all the observed behaviors and movements of its parents and other nearby adults. Tens of millions of movements and gestures had to eventually be identified, interpreted, memorized, and then rehearsed by the youngster, in order to 'speak' with others. Each nuance of a wing flutter, talon lift, neck shake, head bob, or beak articulation—including the gesture's motion, duration, and direction—had to be scrutinized as well as any accompanying crude vocalizations or pupil dilations. No doubt, the mental rigors of such a complex form of communication, provided a cultural drive on the evolutionary development of very big and powerful brains. They had surpassed mankind's abilities long ago and were the only brainy inhabitants to ever develop on Planet Kaarp. Unlike humans, however, they had evolved naturally to become one of the select few apex predators as well, and since they remained such efficient and savage hunters in such a bleak and arid world, they would continue their gruesome but necessary nutritional habits of chomping and swallowing fresh kill or carrion. All this was set into play by evolution long before the advantages their development of technology would later bring. They had also become highly logical and creative beings, with strong senses of compassion, empathy, and social justice. These traits of their collective character were reasons why their society became such a peaceful and successful monoculture—inclusive, supportive, and self-regulating. They were good stewards of their harsh world—protecting and nurturing all the species while maintaining its ecology. Technology was developed and used only as a mean to save lives, improve the planet's ecology, educate or solve societal needs, not for mere convenience and not without first assessing its impact on the environment. Thus, all krrugh practiced frugal, Spartan-like lives as they strived to live in balance with their fellow creatures. They were noble savages.

This was not to say that access to technology was remote, or only for a privileged few because, spread about their arid, sparsely populated, world were ecologically safe, solar-powered techno-kiosks, brimming with all sorts of computers, science supplies, and social media equipment. No kiosk was ever more than 50 miles from anyone, and most krrugh considered such a distance little more than a neighborly stroll. Everything was shared and enjoyed by all, so there was no need of ownership, wealth, business, or commerce. No one did without on Kaarp, as every individual was considered precious and vital to their society, and it was the duty of those more fortunate, somehow, to help and provide for those with less or in need. Truly, the ideals of the krrugh were utopian in scope and nearly so, in practice.

II. Back at the Upper-Deck Viewing Screen

Klaarongah and Krawwgh continued staring at Earth as they stood side-by-side, marveling at the wispy tendrils of white clouds and the deep blue oceans that covered most of its surface. Using one of her three fingers on her left forelimb, Klaarongah pressed a small button and was instantly greeted by a continuous holographic belt displaying all the written symbols of their transcribed dance-language. They both scrutinized all the highlighted symbols and then interpreted the data, which confirmed all the data collected by their scientists quite some time ago. Earth's air was a little lower in oxygen but still readily breathable, without the assistance of any apparatus. Krawwgh, in particular, would be reassured that since the atmospheric pressure was also similar to that on Kaarp, he could adequately swell his lungs as necessary to dive bomb and hunt for prey. Krawwgh saw that Klaarongah's leg was shivering—probably a chill brought about as a side effect of their very long comas. He gently unfurled his huge, soft left wing and skirted it around the lower half of his lover. Instantly luxuriating in his extended feathery-warmth, Klaarongah arched her large graceful neck down to come level with his beak, and gave him a loving eye to eye touch-kiss. Together, they remained at the view screen, admiring Earth and reading the data, when Klaarongah noticed something odd. It was an atmospheric chemical analysis that confirmed anomalously low levels of ozone in the Earth's upper atmosphere, along with a low but persistent and ubiquitous presence of isotopes created by nuclear fission. Immediately they realized that it was a conformation of what they had already learned from their mission log and update service. Earth had recently suffered several nuclear detonations, and as they focused their onboard gamma-camera, they soon learned where. Needing a break from the depressing evidence, they turned off the viewer and left the upper deck to go to the ship's galley and raid the fridge. Relishing their first conscious and solid meal in over six decades, they tore into their thawed klack carcasses as they began reviewing the preparation of the drones.

III. Meanwhile, on Planet Earth...

It had been little more than a decade since the fateful date of 08/08/28 when the People's Republic of China, aided by its newly reacquired ally—the Russian Federation—launched the largest amphibious assault the world had ever seen on the string of islands dotting the South China Sea. This action secured the entire area—and all of its rich fishing and mineral sites for themselves—while also inhibiting the flow of major world shipping lanes. As flagrant and provocative as this action was, it did not spark off a nuclear response. That started three days later as a response by India to a renegade Pakistani general's massive armored assault, on the Indian-controlled province of Jammu-Kashmir. For all the initial destruction and bloodshed caused by the invasion, it paled in comparison to all that would soon follow when, as expected, the enraged Indian Government promptly marshalled a huge response of their own. Soon advancing army divisions and air force sorties from both sides were met and then incinerated by volleys of medium range nuclear ballistic missiles. Many were armed with modern, thermo-nuclear, multi-kiloton warheads. The death, destruction, and misery to follow was unprecedented and unimaginable!

It was desperately hoped that since the world's really big nuclear powers—the United States, Russia, China, France, and Great Britain—'The Big Five' hadn't used any of their own colossal nuclear arsenals, Armageddon had just been avoided. People thought that because all the obvious death and destruction had been localized to the remote, mountainous region between Pakistan and Northern India, the rest of the world had been spared. Sadly, many within the scientific community knew different and forecasted otherwise.

IV. Cloudy, with a Chance of Global Crop Freeze

During their very brief but devastating war, India and Pakistan released approximately 80 nuclear missiles between them. Neither side had come close to exhausting its available arsenal. This had been more than enough, however, to send many millions of tons of very finely pulverized ash high up into the relative calm of the stratosphere. It was here that these light smoky clouds of nuclear war lingered from months to years, as they absorbed and blocked much of the sun's warming rays from reaching the Earth's surface. In only a few months, the dust had spread around the entire Northern Hemisphere, dropping temperatures in some locales by as much as ten degrees Fahrenheit. Coupled to this disastrous phenomena was the many millions of tons of nitrates generated by all the radiation-induced chemical change in the naturally present atmospheric nitrogen. These altered atoms and molecules wreaked havoc on the upper atmosphere's ozone layer, where much of the Sun's dangerous ultra-violet rays were usually attenuated. Now these energetic rays were reaching the Earth's surfaces through the cold, hazy, skies and harmfully irradiating people, crops, and soil. For years to come, these two resulting atmospheric phenomena—known collectively as nuclear winter—would kill over two billion people worldwide, as mass starvation set in because of global crop failures. It was also during this tragic event that an extraterrestrial patience and hope for humanity died, and a merciless mission would begin.

V. Planet 'Kaarp' and the World They Left Behind

Planet Kaarp was a rocky world slightly larger than Earth, that circled an older and smaller yellow star earthlings knew as Tau Ceti, 12 light-years from us. It was closer to its star than Earth, and logically, warmer and drier. It wasn't accompanied by any moons and didn't experience tides or seasons. It did have a stabilized axis, though, because of its position between Tau Ceti and the nearby asteroid belt. Its bulging equator was belted by harsh, colossal deserts, which gave way to sprawling, dry, savannahs before terminating at each pole into red algae matted, and briny, green oceans. It was in the savannahs that planet Kaarp's two species of large herbivores: klacks and gucks, cohabitated. Six feet high at the shoulder, Klacks could weigh over a ton while gucks could attain nearly half that size. They both grazed in the tall thickets of bush grass, which covered much of the savannah.

A tremendous survival opportunity awaited any predators that developed enough power and prowess to take advantage of preying on such large and numerous creatures. As it turned out, the number one predator of these megafauna evolved to become the mighty and brainy krrugh, the giant terror birds of planet Kaarp. Far more effectively than any other massive predator species such as: the powerfully constricting giant marsh snakes, or the rare roaming ocean crocodile, the krrugh became the most efficient predators. Being ten feet tall and weighing 500 pounds, the flightless, bi-pedal ancestors of all modern krrugh had the speed, strength, and cunning to overwhelm and prey upon these large creatures and developed highly effective ambush strategies. If a klack or guck broke free, it wouldn't get very far, as all krrugh possessed cheetah speed and hunted in coordinated packs whenever possible—though a single adult was readily able to take down any of the big prey alone. Although their smaller prehistoric wing appendages had evolved into strong arms with three-fingered hands, it was their powerful hind-limbs terminating into three huge and razor-sharp talons that usually began the life-threatening slashes which spilled the creature's guts. By then, the prey would usually be knocked off its legs, lying on its belly or side helpless, when the krrugh would rear up to its full, stretched-out height, and ram its monstrous, down-tipped dagger of an upper beak into the carcass with bone-crushing force. After killing the prey, the mighty terror bird could then peacefully feast, tearing out huge chunks of its kill and then tilting that monstrous beak skyward, in order to swallow it whole. Since they evolved into social pack hunters, kills were always shared with any other krrugh involved with the hunt first, then any others nearby. If alone with a kill, the hunter would bellow deep honks and caws in order to alert the others in his pack of his position, so that they could enjoy the victorious feast, as klacks and gucks were both big and dangerous.

It was on the grassy spits of sand at the red algae-matted shoreline of the briny polar oceans, that adult krrugh females—accompanied by their mates—came by the thousands to lay their solitary eggs, during their annual cycles. Each mating pair built a mound nearly a foot high from the moist sandy mud and locally selected grass reeds. Then a female would scoop out a hole and deposit her large egg. Now they would patiently wait several days, taking turns sitting on and gently rotating their precious future offspring. The females never left the nest, so it was up to the males to provide meals. This they usually did by dive-fishing in the nearby ocean, or catching some small rodent or crustacean from the surrounding marsh—always sharing their food and parental duties. Finally, that special day would come, and after a strenuous bout of pecking and a chorus of tiny peeps, a hatchling would break free. This truly joyous occasion was immediately tempered by the very demanding parental oversight and vigilance to safeguard the little chicks from the shoreline's many dangers. At least one parent was always awake to watch out for any slithering snakes, lizards, crabs, or scorpions that tried to make beelines for any nest they saw, as attacks could occur at any time—day or night—and from anywhere surrounding them. The toll these creatures took on the hatchlings was noticeable but insignificant, compared to the toll netted by the constant bombardment of the tiny, blood-sucking, screwworm flies, which whenever they found a chick unattended for even a minute, could swarm upon the hapless infant and suck it bone dry. Vastly more hatchlings would succumb to the fly's larvae which, if laid within the chick and not noticed and then painfully plucked out from their tiny bore holes, would quickly grow and start consuming the little hatchling from within. This meant that in addition to all their other brood care duties and regurgitated feedings, parents had to be constantly on the lookout, swatting at the pests and preening their helpless darlings. In step with each breeding season, these flies would pupate within and hatch out of the red algae mats hugging all the shorelines nearby, and then descend by the trillions, on any or all shoreline life, but especially the baby chicks. Within a month, at the end of the breeding season, and despite all the vigilant attention parents could provide, only five to six percent of the hatchlings survived to join their parents on a strenuous thousand-mile journey, back to the deep savannah latitudes where most of the giant herds of klacks and gucks grazed. It was small wonder that they evolved to be so tough, and when coupled to all the mental rigors they went through to develop a language constricted to remembering and interpreting dance moves, they were driven to become the brainiest and mightiest beings on planet Kaarp.

As their species moved through the multitudes of generations, eventually leading up to their current zenith of existence, something rode along with them. Something that at first was infinitesimal in nature. But over the hundreds of millennia, grew to become colossal in impact, and was now threatening their very survival, as a species. Even modern krrugh geneticists couldn't pin down exactly when, or what, was the cause of the startling mutations and transformations that started showing up in krrugh males. A likely culprit would have been a virus, living within those horrible screwworm flies that had plagued them throughout their pre-history. Regardless, at some point in the distant past, a batch of surviving hatchlings must have been infected by a virus or protein that began altering the development of males by shutting down the expression of the normal, relevant genes that regulated the usual krrugh male anatomy, and instead, reactivated many evolutionarily dormant, vestigial genes, sending them down a very different evolutionary path of body structure. In particular, males grew to be much smaller than females, as gradually their legs morphed into very short and stout appendages with enlarged talons, while their forelimbs greatly lengthened and strengthened to change into massive wings enabling them for soaring flight, and a new and effective way to hunt prey. It wasn't that any of these drastic anatomical alterations weakened or lessoned an individual males' chances of surviving and thriving in their dangerous world. Instead, they actually became stronger and better hunters than before, but sadly, less fertile. The resultant reshuffle of dominant genes and their altered locations within the chromatids, made the traits of maleness ever more obscure in their offspring. Although the changes were only minor at first, they accelerated and accumulated throughout time, and eventually resulted in the recently discovered extinction catastrophe. The krrugh race could no longer produce male offspring. They were doomed to completely die out within a couple of generations, unless they could find a compatible species somewhere to mate with, and save as many genetic traits of their dying race as possible, while hoping to create a sentient and fertile, hybrid creature. The zoologist became ecstatic when they first learned about Earth's giant flightless fowl. And again many years later, and well into the voyage of the mission, when their DNA/Protein Spectral Analyzers confirmed the similarities of the ostrich's genome with their own, that the geneticist was finally able to join in the elation with the other scientist. These simple, large birds were in fact their only hope.

The repulsive duty to directly mate with these small-brained, intellectually simple creatures was necessary because any attempts to restrain and artificially inseminate would likely traumatize them, and negatively impact the fragile and vital, inter-species, conception. All things had to be taken into account in order to assure successful fertilization. It was decided that learning about, and then engaging in, natural ostrich mating habits would soothe the beast and offer the best chances for success. While the task weighed heavily on both Klaarongah's and Krawwgh's minds, and neither of them was looking forward to performing the humiliating deeds. But for the sake of their species, they'd do whatever was required, as many times as necessary.

VI. The Pride of Nations Versus the 'Pride' of a World

As much of the Earth's people continued to struggle with mass starvation and frequent outbreaks of disease, they were as usual, completely preoccupied with their own immediate survival and not remotely aware that the world's oceans had acidified as well, which now drove even more species towards extinction. Cagey bureaucrats and politicians dismissed and diminished these claims in attempts to keep panic at a minimum, and everything on an even keel, while selfishly guarding their own plush futures in continued governance.

Hastily tethered truces between many nations were beginning to unravel, as even now, despite the world news media having witnessed and chronicled all the gruesome death and protracted misery circling the globe, people still could not make peace. International empathy and concordance should have been the template by which the world's nations built a more peaceful and tolerant global community. Instead, many of the nations pulled their memberships from the fledgling United Nations, choosing to go alone in their affairs of the world, while radical clergy from all three of the world's monotheisms clamored now, more than ever, that the battle to end all battles had to be fought in order to settle, once and for all, on which faith shall rule and who would be the 'chosen.' Of course, none of them could have known—nor any of their famous prophets from ages' past—that at that very moment, deep in outer space, two vastly superior—but certainly NOT supernatural beings—were planning and preparing for an annihilation of all mankind that no PROPHESY could have foretold.

In orbit around another extra-solar planet, two young, brave, and grimly determined mission specialists were put in their hyper-sleep comas, and then, with an entire world's fervent hopes, safely cocooned into their side-by-side cybernetically monitored chambers for the long journey ahead. All their bodily needs would be continually addressed and attended to. To ward off the effects of micro-gravity that all spacefarers faced, their muscles would be stretched and rigorously exercised several times a day to guard against atrophy, while continual tiny electrical currents would run through their skeletons to inhibit any bone loss. The ship's hull was designed to shield them from all the ultra-high energy cosmic rays that would, otherwise, irradiate and eventually kill them. After their departure from orbit around Kaarp, the onboard medical robots removed all of Klaarongah's and Krawwgh's major internal organs, and placed them in sealed, pressurized containers. Then, they saturated them with a cushioning aero-gel, while assuring that all arteries, veins, and nerves remained anatomically attached to their respective organs and tissues. This was done to ensure that no micro-embolisms or blood clots formed during the tremendous amount of g-forces they would endure, when their vessel was gravitationally slung and centrifugally accelerated by their star to two million miles per hour. This was the ship's shakedown journey, which would subject the massive vessel to its greatest hull stresses while simultaneously charging up all the onboard electro-mechanical systems, as it dipped into Tau Ceti's highly ionized corona. If any catastrophes were waiting to happen, they would likely unfold during this stage of the voyage. Afterwards, the medical robots would vacuum out all the aero-gel and then refit all the organs and their respective tissues back into Klaarongah and Krawwgh, finally laser cauterizing all surgical wounds. By the time the two intrepid star travelers awoke six decades later, there wouldn't be any residual evidence of the drastic surgeries. With the gravitational boost now completed, and their vessel hurtling away from Tau Ceti, the huge array of electro-magnets contained within each of the vessel's drone hulls automatically switched on and ignited the anti-matter catalyzed nuclear fusion drive system, which then continued to accelerate the giant craft for several days, until it had attained one-fifth the speed of light.

At over two miles in diameter and weighing in at just over a million tons, the starship was an astonishing creation. Humanity had come pretty far in its understanding and manipulation of nuclear forces and sub-atomic particles—as sadly evidenced by its recent nuclear war. Their accomplishments in these fields as well as all others of science and technology were tiny in comparison to what the krrugh had achieved. Assembled in a geo-synchronous orbit around Kaarp, whatever materials hadn't already been mined, machined, fabricated, and transported from the process mines scattered about in the nearby asteroid belt, were sky-lifted from the planet's surface onboard giant, orbital sky cranes. They acted like huge orbiting elevators, lifting materials, equipment, and mission personnel up to the starship's assembly platform, as needed. There, they all assembled as dictated by the timing of their critically staged sub-assemblies to build and then launch the vessel. It was comprised of two identical nuclear fusion chambers which also served as the weaponized particle beam accelerators. These were its two drones—each complete—with advanced navigational and autonomous operating systems. At the center of each of the drone's hollow donut-shaped toroidal chambers sat a 100,000 ton nuclear magneton—a gigantic electromagnet of incredible power. Between the tremendous magnetic forces generated by these two central magnetons, as well as those from all the super-cooled magnets wound around each drone's rapidly spinning toroidal fusion chambers, virtually any sub-atomic particles could be crushed and fused together for propulsion energy. It could also be accelerated and focused into powerful weapon beams that could then be targeted through arrayed portals around the ship. In addition to these highly focused particle beams, electro-magnetic radiations, spanning from radio waves to gamma-rays, could be focused or released as directed. Electro-magnetic rays didn't pack nearly as much destructive power as the particle beams, but could be far more penetrating—able to reach inside heavily shielded targets. There was more energy contained in each drone than in all the power plants and hydro-electric damns that had ever operated on Earth. The precise and sophisticated control that each drone possessed, in assessing situations and then discharging their weapons, was bound only by the limits of physics and artificial intelligence. Each drone was really a colossal robot, completely autonomous, able to analyze, comply, and adjust as situations warranted, in order to fulfill their programmed mission objectives. Coupled to the two aligned and overlapping drones was the much smaller but all-important life pod where Klaarongah and Krawwgh would safely reside, hibernate, and then once awoken, oversee the mission. Onboard its computer-managed comfortable quarters, complete with its own fusion propulsion system and analytical labs, the two intrepid mission specialists would receive constant visual updates from each drone as their missions unfolded. Upon learning that humanity was still bristling for war, even after the Indian-Pakistani atrocity, and still continuing to neglect their planet and fellow species, the ruling body of the krrugh became certain that mankind needed to be exterminated. From then on, only a command issued by the mission control center could alter or stop the drones from carrying out their genocidal missions which was loaded long ago into their respective computer banks.

Except for all the necessary electro-magnetic materials and systems, the entire starship was constructed out of the strongest and lightest non-ferrous alloys and engineered carbon nano-materials, in order to assure supreme rigidity and shielding. This was necessary in order to protect the crew and all the sensitive equipment from the two drone chamber's constant, pulsed oscillations of their powerful magnetic fields, as well as the integrity of the giant vessel itself, which would have imploded, if it were made of ferrous or other magnetizing elements, the instant it switched on. On the outer-most surfaces of the super-magnetized and rapidly spinning toroids—those donut-shaped plasma and weapon beam chambers of the two drones—accreted over time, all the space gas and dust residues encountered as the ship traveled through interstellar areas of frozen comet gases, such as those found in our solar system's colossal Oort cloud, or its large asteroid belt's tiny grains of dust. This was anticipated and would present no problems for the drones. In time, the several-foot thick layer of accreted material would serve to further increase vessel hull strength, provide greater radiation shielding for crew and sensitive equipment, and supply extra source material to be consumed as fuel for the ship's propulsion or beam weaponry. During their own space age, the krrugh learned that no factor of a vessel's construction, operation, or potential encounters could afford to be overlooked or under-utilized, and every aspect of a mission had to mesh perfectly, for assured success.

Just as impressive as all the material, engineering, and technology that was invested in the vessel was the staggering amount of training and education Klaarongah and Krawwgh received, in preparation for the mission. Being exceptional even among their other mission candidates meant that they both devoured their course loads and tirelessly rehearsed all their training, until they both had mastered everything necessary from nuclear-particle physics and planetary ecology to species preservation theory and molecular biology. They underwent rigorous psychological and sociological training as well, to anticipate, recognize, and compensate for any exhibited mood swings, loss-of-focus, or other mission jeopardizing behaviors in themselves or one another. To them, it only strengthened their love and will for a successful mission. They continually reminded themselves and reassured the entire mission team that the mission would always come first. Humbled, they also understood that as nearly flawless as the vessel's design was—with all its built-in redundancy and safety features—as well as the careful analysis and alternate planning for unseen contingencies arising during the mission, THEY WERE THE MISSION'S WEAKEST LINKS! If the mission should fail somehow, it would be because of them. Knowing that, they descended into their black, dreamless, sleeps while the decades and light-years ticked on by. Guided by their world's steadfast resolve, they unconsciously hurtled ever onward, to awaken and then rain 'stellar-assured destruction' down upon the foolish and flawed inhabitants of the blue jewel world, planet Earth!

VII. Wakey, Wakey!

Nearly 60 years later, as measured by the dying krrugh on planet Kaarp, and neglecting the time dilation effects of special relativity as experienced by the vessel and her crew, the shipboard mission management computer revived Klaarongah and Krawwgh, steered clear of asteroid collisions, and guarded her disclosure from Earth—still some 150 million miles away. The computer's navigational auto-pilot selected a ten-mile-wide asteroid and then sidled up to its far-Earth side, in order to hide behind it. It then measured and logged in its mass, g-forces, and orbit among the asteroids, to continuously monitor and adjust the ship's thrusters and maintaining its position, hiding behind the huge boulder for as long as necessary. Afterwards, the computer launched a little crawler probe which scrambled over the asteroid's craggy surface to the opposite, Earth-facing side. At the right ascension and declination points for best viewing Earth, the probe exploded, causing four wire-bobbins to immediately unfurl a gossamer-thin wire mesh over a ten square-meter area, then embed and anchor their hard, pointy-spikes into the surface. Within a minute, the sensitive receiver was picking up and honing in on TV and radio broadcasts from Earth.

As Klaarongah and Krawwgh finished reviving from their comas, they began reviewing any of the mission sent message-traffic, as well as all the heart-warming family social banter and announcements of life-marker events in their loved one's lives, to sadly include the deaths of most of them. After their own startling confirmation of their middle-aged bodies, and sorely missed slept-through youths, they briefly trysted, before luxuriating under a shower, together. As they somberly reflected on the facts of how far away they were in both space and time from any of their family and friends, they both knew only too well that any signals they sent would never reach anyone alive. Clearly, their communications could be one way only. Just one character symbol message had been sent from the Mission Control Center without any updates since its arrival, nearly two decades earlier. *'Study Earth at a safe and clandestine distance, while remaining undetected and minimizing panic for as long as possible. When in position, authorize drones to attack and remediate. Then, if possible, attempt species hybridization and colonization. Thanks, we remain proud of you, and hopeful for a successful mission. Best Wishes and Much Love, MC!'*

Still cuddled close together as they stared at the ominous but hopeful message while mulling over all the implications and marveling on how brief and non-specific it was regarding methods and timetables, they both reasoned that the mission commanders must truly trust in the drones' capabilities as well as themselves. The fact that it had been sent pretty long ago, with no more recent updates, could mean only one thing. Even though there had been careful planning to assure mission continuity with younger staff members filling in, while the older ones died off, they were now all dead. This gave them both a mixed feeling of fear and pride. Pride in the hopeful confidence the mission control members had in Klaarongah's and Krawwgh's abilities and will to see it all through, but fear in the realization that they were totally alone now, and it was ALL UP TO THEM!

As always, it was Klaarongah who flicked off the computer screen because it was her sex whose forelimbs remained powerful arms, terminating into articulated wrists and palms complete with three long, strong, and dexterous fingers. In the society of the krrugh, most females were the medical doctors, engineers, and technicians where their dexterity was a necessity, while all the winged males—including Krawwgh—became theoreticians, scientists, and project overseers on all their joint projects, together. Despite the drastic differences in their anatomies brought forth as a result of the assault on their genetic makeup so long ago, they had used their keen wits and social empathy to make the best of things and thus, over time, culturally evolved to become a race of highly cooperative and complimentary creatures. Whether it was hunting for food or building interstellar spaceships, all Krrugh knew that no matter what an individual's abilities were, they were always much more effective and efficient when paired together—especially as male and female. And so, as Klaarongah got busy, physically setting up all the necessary holographic laser equipment with all their switches and display pads, Krawwgh carefully studied and reviewed the chronology of events to unfold and what to expect when they would finally RELEASE THE DRONES.

VIII. Release the Drones

A few hours later, they were ready. Klaarongah sat down on her nest cushion chair while Krawwgh waddled over and climbed up onto his perch besides her. Immediately, two visor helmets descended from their ceiling compartments and settled on their heads. Now, they were neurologically netted to the entire ship, its onboard computer, all the shipboard telemetry, and lastly, the drones. They were still hovering behind the large asteroid some 150 million miles from Earth. Each drone's toroid directionally counter-spinning with respect to the other's and, thus, providing axial stability and up until now, swinging the comparatively small life pod around just fast enough for its centrifugal force to simulate gravity for Klaarongah and Krawwgh. When the life pod slowed to a stop and its artificial gravity ceased, the two alien astronauts strapped themselves in, and the life pod suddenly took a ride on one of the ship's huge, automated hull plates and slid to a position dead center above the upper of the two much larger drones.

Having authorized the onboard mission computer to execute this next phase of the mission, the two of them sat anxiously as the computer took over all the activities. Several explosive bolts fired simultaneously, freeing the two drones from each other and the life pod, which was still attached to its separated hull plate, as the drones descended several miles below the main horizontal plane of the asteroid belt in order to avoid any collisions with asteroids, or other orbital debris. Once they reached the designated coordinates, the two huge discs spun up their already fully charged toroids and torched off their plasma rockets as they instantly accelerated to one-fifth, the speed of light. At such an immense velocity, they would reach Earth's big solo moon within 15 minutes. Klaarongah and Krawwgh continued watching the drones' progress through their helmet visors, admiring their tiny but pronounced spectral red shifts that glowed brightly in the visor's prism lens, as they receded away from them at such high speed. Soon, the data signals from each drone would reach them, and they would be able to see what the drones were actually doing.

They watched the telemetry returning from the drones and checked the onboard mission computer for any signs of human responses that might signal detection. All things were going smoothly, and they saw none. The beginning attack would unfold far too fast for any of mankind's surveillance satellites to detect until it was too late. As for Klaarongah and Krawwgh, they would remain safely hidden until the drones had completed their specific mission objectives. Slowly, Klaarongah floated up from her cushion nest and began bending and stretching her massive legs and arms, while Krawwgh began unfurling and stretching his huge wings in the weightless environs. It wasn't easy for such athletic hunters to remain still for long sessions, especially after enduring such a long hyper-sleep.

In order for the two drones too shed much of their stellar-travel velocity, so that they could survive their encounter with Earth's atmosphere, and then eventually hover within it, each drone had to successfully complete an instant and exacting 180 degree flip about its vertical axis. If the maneuver was performed flawlessly, the NOW oppositely directed spin of the toroid on each drone would immediately begin exerting a huge drag on its forward velocity, rapidly slowing the drone down to a much safer, planet-approaching, speed. The challenge was getting the gigantic discs to flip instantly and exactly 180 degrees—one-half a revolution about its vertical axis. If the maneuver was done too slowly, or if the flip over or under-shot the true vertical position, then either or both drones—each with their toroids still spinning at thousands of revolutions per minute—would be shredded to bits in a colossal explosion by perturbations within each disc's titanic centrifugal forces.

Still, some 300,000 miles out from the moon, the two drones automatically lined up single-file as they approached.

Hiding directly behind the moon from Earth's view meant that if something did go wrong, it would likely remain out of sight and only crash on the far side of the moon, where any space debris generated would remain. Klaarongah reached out and grabbed a tuft of Krawwgh's wing feathers, as they both sat motionless, not even breathing as the countdown began. The very instant the countdown ended, powerful jets erupted simultaneously on opposite ends of each drone with one jet topside while the other, at bottom. Simultaneously, the two drones flipped in unison, and successfully stabilized their vertical axes. Krawwgh confirmed what they had breathlessly watched. The telemetry reports from both drones came in and showed they were dead center vertical, and still on course, decelerating in a rapid and predictable manner. As he sat there, peering over the reassuring data pouring in from each drone, he knew that soon the drones would approach the moon, with one drone going over its North Pole while the other would go over the South Pole, to begin their sneak attack on Earth. By choosing the extreme polar trajectories to Earth, the mission planners surmised that it would result in the least probability of being detected while approaching from space and the slowest route to spark widespread panic among the world's militaries and populace. Within minutes, there would be no further need for continued secrecy as by then, both drones would already be over both of Earth's poles, gliding very high in the stratosphere and obliterating any pre-selected targets, while simultaneously exterminating all of humanity. No one, nor anything, would be able to interfere.

Both of them were still elated by the successful completion of the drone flips, and Krawwgh's ever-persistent appetite was grabbing his attention. Klaarongah was still studying the two drone's decreasing velocities as they approached the moon.

She bobbed her head in awe as she witnessed their red shifts wink out.

Possessing the necessary appendages, she was temporarily stuck at her post—manning all the command switches and emergency abort buttons—while Krawwgh gave into his hunger and hopped off of his perch and floated over to the huge walk-in refrigerator. Even though he was less than half as big as Klaarongah, the extreme musculature of his aerial physique required twice as much daily caloric intake as hers so it was only natural that he would have to eat much more per day. Using his beak, he unlatched the vacuum-sealed vault-door and entered. Immediately to his right, on a low-lying shelf, was a scrumptious-looking flank of freeze-dried guck. Instinctively, he stabbed his rock-hard, pointy beak into the semi-frozen flesh. He repeated this a couple of times until he had reamed a big hole in the flank, then he pried open his beak and chomped down, tearing out a big chunk in the process, before swallowing it whole. He fed until he was stuffed, and then he left the fridge and floated over to the shower. As he sat drinking and luxuriating under the vacuum-assisted spray, his selfish preoccupation gave way to concerns about his lover and fellow astronaut, who was still busily scanning the heavens and manning the switches. He spryly floated back to his perch, which for once, put him at a higher seated elevation than his loving but distracted mate. He lowered his beak and gently stroked the side of it against Klaarongah's throat and under-beak, signaling that he had something for her. She softly cawed out a 'thank you' and then tilted and opened her huge beak like a tiny hatchling to receive and relish her generously regurgitated meal. Krrugh's were supremely sophisticated beings, yet simply savage birds, when hunting or dining!

A visual and audio alarm began blinking and pinging which indicated the time was very near when the drones' trajectories would separate, carrying one over and the other under the moon. They would continue on towards their polar positions to begin their coordinated attacks on Earth—just over an hour from now. Putting his visor helmet back on, Krawwgh joined Klaarongah viewing the series of awe-inspiring visions of this prominent moon, so singular, large, and spherical. It shone with crystal-like clarity, as it's prehistoric impact craters and shadowy valleys revealed it's violent past while brightly glowing in sharp, colorless, sun-lit contrast to the deep blackness of space. Having evolved on a moonless world, they could only imagine what it was going to be like to experience Earth's short, distinct seasons, moon-tugged ocean tides, and much longer days and nights. Existing at an optimal distance from her sun to receive enough light and heat for liquid water and photosynthesis, while possessing a large, nearby moon to stabilize its spin axis and slow its revolutions, it was small wonder that once it started, so much life evolved and thrived on this fortuitous and bountiful world!

IX. They Came out of Nowhere

Each drone had been programmed to seek out the brightest star of their respective hemispheres, as viewed from Earth, and then align their approach with that star's highest flux of Earthbound light rays, so that their own glowing hulls would be nearly invisible to any ground-based observatories. Still rapidly decelerating from over 200,000 miles per hour, ($1/670^{th}$) of their original relativistic stellar-traveling speed, they hurtled by and pulsed powerful short bursts of X-rays in order to incinerate any high orbiting geo-synchronous military surveillance satellites they encountered, such as those of the United States and Russia's space commands, while vectoring to their respective polar coordinates. Once reached, each drone signaled the other and synchronized it's mission-elapse timers, while simultaneously pulsing all relevant strategic information to the life pod, where Klaarongah and Krawwgh were anxiously waiting and ready to receive all the drones' situational status reports and visual data streams. All systems were go!

At 2:37:53 am, Greenwich Mean Time (GMT), on 06/27/2076 A.C.E., both drones left their respective low-orbit, polar hovering coordinates and began their genocidal attacks while the United States, Russia, and China scrambled to assess what was happening. As it swooped down to within 15 miles of Earth's surface, Drone#1, tuned in on all the radar sweeps and radio communications chatter, emanating from a NORAD post off the coast of northern Labrador, Canada. Taking only milliseconds to analyze and confirm its militaristic functions, the drone then pulsed an intense blue beam of high-energy protons into the huge radar dish immediately overloading and shorting out its electronics and melting the dish. Panicked at the sudden realization that they were under some form of attack, all the radar crew scrambled out of the two buildings only to see a tiny reddish 'cigar' very high in the sky. One among them raised his binoculars in the object's direction when a lovely, pinkish-orange hue filled his eyes followed by an instant, intense burst of searing pinpricks, then nothing. He and all his fellow crew of Canadian Royal Air Force buddies had just been optically dilated by the neurologically relaxing hue, then killed instantly as a tremendous flux of infra-red photons showered down all around them, piercing their optical nerves and frying their brains! Meanwhile Drone#2 had set upon a Norwegian Antarctic Weather Station and took its turn proton-melting the facility while optically 'pink-frying' the brains of anyone outdoors. As both drones began their particle and photon bombardments, they simultaneously released a highly persistent and species-specific nerve agent which was lethal to humans only. It was a remarkably stable compound—able to kill by inhalation or exposed skin, and being heavier than air, assured an inevitable human contact. This agent was synthesized by the automated life pod laboratories during the long stellar voyage to Earth. As soon as they were close enough to Earth, sensitive bio-spectrometers could locate, analyze, data-store and then chemically recreate virtually any organic molecule existing on the planet. Almost any area was suitable for analysis because so much of Earth's surface was awash in excreta or other materials from living things—especially human beings. As expected from vastly superior minds with such a purposeful culture guided by science and reason, the krrugh had planned a multi-pronged approach to humanity's extermination. They could readily disintegrate, lethally irradiate, burn, fry, or poison anyone or anything with remarkable precision. There would be NO PLACES TO HIDE!

While the extermination of mankind was the primary focus of the drones' missions, the others were: elimination of all his toxic, pollution-generating technologies, remediation of the severely damaged global ecology, and the protection and preservation of all the varieties of life-forms. As the extermination began, collateral damage and death to other species was minimized as much as possible, and usually limited to only the death or injury of pets and service animals because of their close proximity to humans. Every effort in mission planning and drone execution was made to spare all non-human life and wildlife, especially any species identified as endangered and rare. So, simultaneous to all the death and destruction the drones would rain down on the Earth, they would be constantly removing pollutants from the atmosphere, hydrosphere and lithosphere, while replenishing depleted substances such as nitrogen and ozone. All this was to be done to restore Earth's natural ecology.

Only moments after the detection and destruction of the NORAD radar base, Drone#1 detected a Russian Federation nuclear ballistic missile submarine lurking off the coast of Maine. Since it had so much fissile material contained within its nuclear reactor and all the ballistic missile warheads onboard, instead, the drone selected to pulse a powerful and penetrating beam of neutrons down on the unsuspecting sub, trawling hundreds of meters beneath the waves. This powerful dose of radiation instantly killed the crew while it also induced atom-splitting chain reactions in all the onboard fissile materials resulting in a massive nuclear explosion. Hereafter, whenever either drone detected any fissile materials anywhere on Earth, whether contained in a vessel, weapon, missile silo, power reactor, or stored on a base somewhere, they pulsed the penetrating neutron beams until they had induced the inevitable nuclear detonations, and resultant loss of lives. Not only was this removing mankind's most plausible threat of a retaliatory response against the drones, it also completely destroyed one of life's most dangerous and enduring pollutants, ultra-poisonous and long-lived radioactive isotopes.

As for launching any missiles at or directing any jetfighter sorties against either drone all responses proved futile! A U.S. Air Force base, scrambled a squadron of hyper-sonic, stealth fighters at Drone#1 which was following its pre-programmed, circumpolar mission. Neither fighter groups could fly as high as the drone's planned operational altitude, and before they could get within range to effectively fire their missiles, the drone detected them. Once they were within an optimal range to destroy while also minimizing damage to the ecology, the drone pulsed an array of protons and X-rays that destroyed the squadron and pre-detonated each jet's compliment of weapons—conventional or otherwise. Then, the victorious drone spun up its toroid chamber—which had a deep-red glow because of the friction it generated in the atmosphere—and vacuumed up all the debris left over. This action not only cleared the local air but also provided extra material for the drone to use as fuel. Matter and energy were never wasted by the krrugh. The last thing all the brave pilots noticed before being incinerated in a blinding, brilliant-blue flash was that the previously reported reddish-silver 'cigar' was actually a gigantic, flying saucer with a red-glowing rim.

Since either drone was able to carry out its attacks with such power and precision from such high altitudes, they were untouchable. Even if somehow, a sneak attack against either of them happened, the weapon used as well as the energy it contained would assuredly be neutralized and then adsorbed onto the toroid's spinning and semi-molten surfaces. This fearful fact applied to missiles, rockets, propelled bombs and grenades, high-powered projectiles—ANYTHING humanity could come up with! By the end of the first day, over half a billion humans had been killed. Several dozen ICBM silos and nuclear subs had been hunted down and destroyed, along with numerous jetfighter squadrons. On the plus side—for Earth if not humanity—the drones were vacuuming-up huge amounts of carbon dioxide and other greenhouse gases while synthesizing and sending quantities of UV-ray protective ozone into the upper atmosphere. Even some of the lingering, pulverized dust created nearly 50 years earlier by the Indian-Pakistani nuclear war was absorbed and utilized by the two drones. Truly, the drones would make the Earth a better place—WITHOUT HUMANS.

X. Huddled Someplace Secret and Deep

At a secret location, under 900 feet of mountain granite inside a nuclear blast-proof bunker sat Republican President Phillip T. Thompson and most of his cabinet members. They were huddled around a large, oval table. Washington DC along with most of the eastern seaboard, lay in apocalyptic ruin with untold millions dead as the combinations of deadly rays and species-specific nerve-gas took their grim toll. The only survivors were those not yet encountered by the drones. A large number of primary government and military members had not escaped the attacks on Congress or the Pentagon, and as news kept filtering in on the ever-escalating mayhem, folks were beginning to lose it. The president reached out and clasped the hands of his two nearest cabinet members and softly uttered, "C'mon folks! I know we've all been through a lot but we have got to keep it together. Our country is depending on us!" Sobs died down, and the room grew quiet in order to regroup and think. Then, the president turned to his Science Advisor, Bill Kadlowski, as he returned to the table after getting some coffee. "What do you have on all this, Bill, and what can we do to stop the hellish things?"

Lowering his head in thoughtful contemplation as he analyzed the dire question he took a sip and looked the president in the eyes. "Sir, what little intel that's trickled back has come from several fighter pilots right before they died. I'm sad to say it doesn't look good for us."

Trying to keep his own level of growing despair from becoming obvious in his next question, the president continued. "Now, when you say us…you mean the United States?"

"I mean everybody! All of humanity," Bill flatly responded. Murmurs and small gasps erupted again. "T-That can't be true, Bill. I mean, c'mon, there's only two of them, after all!" Bill again thoughtfully paused as he remembered how uninformed and suspicious the overtly religious commander-in-chief was on most matters of science and technology, so he carefully phrased his response. "Respectfully, sir, you don't understand. These things use energy like nothing ever witnessed on Earth. They seem to be able to literally absorb anything we throw at them. Then they immediately return fire on Americans or Russians. Remember that sub?"

"Oh, come off it, Bill, there must be something. What about a really big nuke? You know, one of those multi-megatoners? Didn't you once tell me nothing can withstand the biggest ones?"

Chagrinned that the president only chose to remember the weapon's power and not its cumbersome size, as well as all the inherent dangers encountered when staging and arming such old devices, Bill struggled to remain respectful but factually accurate, as he answered. "Yes, sir. In theory, nothing less dense than a neutron star could withstand a direct hit, but the fighters have already fired a couple of our smaller ones at it, and all I know for certain is that after all the smoke cleared the brave fighters and all their ordinance were gone—

DISINTEGRATED—while the saucer remained apparently unfazed and continued on."

The president sat silently for several seconds as he mulled over HIS plans. Finally he continued. "Well now…here's what we'll do. I'll talk to one of the ICBM silo commanders and have him load up their biggest bastards on a couple of our rockets while we continue to get updates on its position and where it seems to be going. Bill, didn't you say it looked like it was on some North Pole route?"

"The one we've been engaged with is, sir, but the other one seems to be running on a corkscrewing horizontal route, parallel with the equator."

"I wonder why they're doing that?" asked the president.

Bill emitted a sigh. "It's just a guess on my part, sir, but it may be a way of assuring double-coverage so they don't miss anything. Or anybody." The gruesome conjecture left the room stunned and silent for a good minute or more. Then the president picked up the hot phone while an assigned agent handed him the special attaché case known as the football, which connected the president with Strategic Defense Command, so that he could issue the go codes authorizing the launch of any of the nation's nuclear arsenal. He then talked directly with an air force general in charge of an array of ICBM silos in southeast Wyoming. Despite receiving even more misgivings about using any antique cold war weapons that the cabinet science advisor had already counseled against only moments earlier, the obviously annoyed commander-in-chief politely but firmly insisted that the general make haste and mate the biggest warheads with whatever rockets still capable of performing the job. He then briskly slammed the phone down and placed his elbows on the table to bury his weary face in his big hands. While the president silently sat there resting his eyes, Bill nervously slurped his coffee, struggling to hide his continually growing disappointment in the president and his stubborn unwillingness to take expert advice. To him, the president was little more than a cowboy preacher, a social tyrant certain in his God-guided righteousness in all matters regarding his office and how he chose to run the country. Bill was snapped back to attention when the president began clearing his throat to speak. What he said next would almost bring his sanity into question as far as the Atheist scientist and engineer was concerned.

The President began. "I know that many of you are serious Christians like myself." He paused to let the controversial praise please most of his politically conservative staff as he looked around the table. "It has occurred to me through spiritual revelation that if this really is to be 'The Beginning of the End of Days' as foretold in the Christian Bible, we'd better have a backup plan. If this is that 'moment of Divine judgment' we can face it. We have to. So with whatever means of mass media we have left in alliance with ALL our Christian ministries and televangelist connections, we have to convince our fellow Americans—and the rest of the world—that this is a hopeful AND INEVITABLE transformation for all of humanity as God's will on Earth and accept it. Then, when all the dying is done, OUR SAVIOR JESUS CHRIST will descend into our midst and redeem the worthy among us to sit at the foot of His throne in Heaven."

Hoping no one else noticed, the science advisor rolled his eyes and stifled a derisive groan on hearing such simple-minded drivel. As a former top-level manager of the National Nuclear Security Administration (NNSA), as well as an expert nuclear engineer, he was educated and trained to use empirical scientific methodology and logical reasoning to pose questions then search for their answers—not to accept ancient, superstitious dogmas championed through time by the overtly religious and overly gullible. As he remembered the bible from his own Lutheran youth, the extraterrestrial DOOMSDAY being rained down upon them now was nothing like any prophesy he had read in the bible or anywhere else. Grimly hearing only dribs and drabs about the annihilation of the fighter squadrons, missile bases and submarines already encountered by the drones, he knew better than anyone just how hopeless and pointless our military responses were proving to be. He remembered that several of the first fighter jet pilots had tried desperately to hail the aliens onboard the craft, but to no avail. Bill noticed each of the vessel's adherence to their respective longitudes and latitudes with faultless computer-like precision. A cold shudder ran through him as he pondered, for the first time, the possibility that the two colossal alien death weapons might be drones, whose creators were likely too far away to hear or care about any offered surrender terms or pleas for mercy.

Just then his reflections were shattered when the president—who had already risen from his seat and started consoling and bolstering his fellow Christian cabinet members with hugs and back slaps—came up behind him and began giving a less-than-gentle neck massage. As his big hands painfully rolled and kneaded Bill's understandably tight shoulders, he whispered through a smug, condescending smile. "You see how it's done, Billy? You've got to distract them while also offering them hope. And to that end, the facts don't really matter. Sometime later today the big nukes will either work or they won't. And if not, I've already started the people's acceptance of the impending dread as divine will, and hope for the heavenly judgment to come. Either way, I win."

Disgusted beyond description at what the president had just whispered in his ear, Bill slowly rose from his seat to look the grinning and duplicitous bastard in the eye, when it happened.

Staying dead true to its circumpolar flight plan around Earth, Drone#1 had already lapped the Earth twice in the hour and a half since it had destroyed Washington DC and all the other east coast megacities along similar longitudes when it picked up on a televised broadcast emanating from several dispersed sources. It was the soon to be killed president of the United States, pleading for a merciful cessation of hostilities while also threatening with an as yet unseen, retaliatory response. The drone honed in on a very small but intense stream of gamma-rays emanating from what it determined to be a small nuclear reactor at the base of a mountain near the Allegany-Green Ridge range in Maryland. Because of the krrugh's decades-long study of all of humanity's activities and communications, there were no military or political secrets they didn't already know. There were no weapons, military strategies, base locations, or secret hideaways they didn't already have at least some knowledge about. In less than a minute, the onboard data banks identified it as the location of the above-ground back-up power system for a secret nuclear defense bunker 900 feet below. Sensing that it was drawing in air, for the bunker, the drone assessed the flow rate and likely underground volume of air then released a small rocket-canister of nerve gas. It landed close to the air intakes and emitted puffs of the invisible, odorless gas down the ventilation shafts. Instantly, the president and his terrified cabinet members began twitching and jerking about violently before suddenly collapsing. This alien agent had easily made it through the bunker's atomic, biological and chemical air defense filters and killed them all in just under two minutes!

Even before the attack began, both drones had been continuously broadcasting their respective video streams back to Klaarongah and Krawwgh still in the distant comfort and security of the life pod hidden behind the big asteroid. For the first time ever, viewing humanity in vivid, visual detail, they marveled at what strangely beautiful creatures they appeared to be and were saddened at what had to be done to them as they watched the president's futile plea and simultaneous threat of retaliation on the dance-interpreted visor screen of their pilot helmets. They carefully scrutinized the movements of the little figurines gyrating and wriggling from the corners of their vision fields dancing-out the pathetic human's vacuous, oral language. The startling differences in anatomies between humans and other apes fascinated Klaarongah and Krawwgh. Humans had large heads and flat faces. Obviously evolved for walking instead of swinging and climbing through trees, they were upright and tall with long-striding legs, shortened arms, and small hands that became highly dexterous when freed from the rigors of locomotion. As the two bird-beings skimmed through the evolutionary and cultural pop-up holographic files regarding homo-sapiens, they learned that their disproportionately large brains made them intelligent and fully sentient, but also very delusional. They saw agency in everything, which fueled a lot of creativity, but also fueled superstition at the expense of reason, and made most of them unable to learn much more about themselves and their marvelous world after attaining adulthood.

Nowhere was this more evident than in what they had done to their world and so many of their fellow inhabitants. In most of their actions, inactions, and previous feeble attempts to address these globally important issues, they were a total menace. Largely uncaring and politically incompetent at acknowledging the threats they posed to the environment and their fellow species—let alone, organizing the will to stop them. They couldn't care because they were preoccupied with themselves and their continual self-inflicted miseries.

As the human-generated broadcast abruptly ended, Klaarongah and Krawwgh sat quietly, dismayed and disgusted by what they'd seen, not only in the arrogant president's transmission, but at the continuous footage of videos streaming in on all the environmental degradation so obviously present. They both hoped the mission had arrived in time to save this planet from its first ever unnatural mass extinction. After the extermination of mankind, only time could tell whether or not all the other threatened species would rebound.

All this troublesome contemplation was put on hold as an updated data stream poured in from Drone#2. They watched with grim detachment as it came up on the shores of southern Brazil and began lethally pink frying the brains of many beach goers. A brilliant indigo bolt, with a resulting bluish flash, followed by a thunderous blast indicated that a local nuclear power plant had been detonated as well. Krawwgh noticed the immediate increase in alpha, beta, gamma, and neutron radiation levels, resulting from the release of billions upon billions of radioactive atoms formerly contained within the now-destroyed reactor's fuel rods on the drone's environmental radiation monitor but knew he need not worry, because the drone would return and remediate the nuclear disaster by scooping up and then incorporating all the atmospheric debris. Meanwhile, Klaarongah was still studying the corpses left back on the beach and winced with a female's instinctual empathy as she saw the now lifeless tiny arms and legs of two toddlers, peeking out from beneath the body of their mother, who had likely gathered them under herself in a hopeless, last-ditch effort to save and console them. Instantly sensing Klaarongah's natural distress at seeing such a thing, Krawwgh gently enfolded her in a soothing wing embrace. They both knew they were still quite early in the mission with many more disturbing images yet to come.

Just before 6:00 p.m. Central Time, after the total decimation and destruction of Detroit and all its inhabitants, a hastily prepared 110-year-old liquid oxygen-fueled Minuteman Three was launched and well on its way to intercept Drone#1. Within the missile's special nose cone sat a single, two and a half ton W41, a 25 MEGATON warhead, the most powerful nuclear weapon the United States ever possessed. None of her previous iterations had ever been detonated, only component tested and rated. She was the very last one in the US nuclear arsenal and over 100 years of age as well. No one still alive had ever worked on her or any following editions, so she was cobbled and packaged together by instruction book-guided air force missile assembly technicians as carefully as possible, with a newer, less-sensitive but more powerful explosive lens surrounding her physics package. If all went according to plan, she would detonate within half a mile or so of the space saucer and subject it to the crumpling pressure of billions of times normal atmosphere and nearly one hundred million degrees of heat. The thinking was that at this level of explosive power, she could be even a couple of miles off-target and still deliver a fatal blow!

At 6:07 p.m., the missile reached the highest point of its near orbital arc, and the special, super-hardened, laser-shielding bus that housed the warhead successfully separated from the massive booster-rocket and was on track to intercept its target in five minutes. In truth, some sort of super-sonic cruise-missile would have been stealthier, but they couldn't begin to fly nearly as fast, far, or high—and more importantly, none of them ever built by anybody on Earth could carry such a big payload. At precisely 6:10:30 p.m., Central Time, the drone instantly pulsed a series of neutron beams at the warhead—still ninety-some miles above the target. Since the beams were not composed of the light photons contained in all lasers but were instead a very dense concentration of comparatively massive and uncharged particles, no type of shielding could keep them from penetrating and inducing nuclear fissions inside the weapon's two compartments—both of which contained large quantities of fissile materials. As pre-planned by the drone to minimize what would have otherwise resulted in massive atmospheric and environmental radioactive contamination and unnecessarily harmed many life-forms, the warhead exploded with all of its colossal force but still high above the Earth and nowhere near the target! As the intel report on the missile's failure reached the air force missile commander, confirming what he surely already knew, while also dashing his last remaining hope for a miracle, he uttered a soft 'thank you' and hung up. Nothing on Earth could stop the two extra-terrestrial vessels, and by the end of the day, ALL nuclear material on earth, including nuclear power plants, research reactors, high-energy particle accelerators, laser research centers, and any stores of nuclear weapons or fissionable materials had been fissioned-up and forever consumed. For the first time in over a 130 years NOBODY on Earth had a nuclear weapon or the critical materials with which to build one. As they efficiently continued their missions, both drones occasionally encountered radio-contacts pleading to be spared as well as desperate fighter jet attacks. Hours earlier, Drone#1 was flying high over Siberia on its continuous circumpolar flight about to annihilate the last of the Russian Federation's missile defense silos when it encountered a sortie of Russian fighters. As expected, the jets launched a barrage of conventional rockets at the drone which responded by pre-detonating the warheads and incinerating the jets. Then, it swept up and accreted all the resulting debris onto the red-hot, semi-molten surfaces of its rapidly spinning toroid. One last-ditch effort involved a lone pilot trying to somehow sneak into range and release a rocket carrying a latest generation nerve agent called 'novichok' in a desperate bid that maybe the stuff would get sucked in somehow and poison the 'alien genocidal bastards' they thought might lurk within the monstrous thing, but again to no avail. He, his jet, and the poison were instantly obliterated, and all the debris was once again swept up by the pilotless drone!

XI. First Glimpses of Hope!

Throughout the last couple of Earth's long days and nights, the drones relentlessly continued their liquidation of humanity, while simultaneously renewing Earth's heavily polluted atmosphere. Other restorative efforts would have to wait until the arrival of Klaarongah and Krawwgh on the life pod. Most of Earth's natural replenishment would occur after the extermination of mankind, when its own ecological forces would no longer be constantly compromised by continuous human exploitation. When the drones began their fateful missions, they had a global census of human population at just over a disastrous nine billion. It had been over eleven billion before the Indian-Pakistani nuclear war, which then caused a global nuclear winter, starving some two billion people to death in the years that followed!

Since the beginning of their genocidal mission, not even two full days earlier, the drones had killed nearly five billion people—over half the world's remaining population. Because most of the heavily weaponized countries existed in the Northern Hemisphere, Drone#1 had been much busier engaging and destroying military challenges than Drone#2, which instead spent more time pink-frying and nerve-gassing multitudes of dispersed villagers, desert-dwellers, and the poor jungle tribes throughout South America, Australia, and Africa. Drone#2 also had more time to collect and analyze environmental samples and conduct species investigations. It was in Equatorial Africa when it first noticed large ostriches, and in Ethiopia and Somalia when it located the largest species, *STRUTHIO CAMELUS*, the biggest birds on Earth and the ones deemed worthy of attempted hybridization. Identifying all areas where these ostriches were sighted and then logging the coordinates, Drone#2 immediately alerted Drone#1 to avoid using its weapons in those areas to assure the protection of the precious birds. This action would likely allow some very small populations of humans to live, but the two mission specialists would be able to deal with that problem.

The enhanced data and video streams reached Klaarongah and Krawwgh 15 minutes later, and both of them gawked at a small fleeing group of the big birds, which were probably evading a cheetah or lion. Even from over 15 miles of altitude, the drone was easily capable of zooming in on the individuals of the pack. As Krawwgh concentrated on all the collected physiological and biochemical data, Klaarongah focused instead on the individual creatures—especially a pregnant female—as the drone conducted a continuous scan of the speedy creatures. Peering at her belly, Klaarongah was pleased to notice a thick, sturdy shell forming around the large, healthy-looking embryo, knowing it wouldn't be too long before the mother nested and laid her very large egg. They both were pleased to see how strong and healthy they all appeared to be, and how hopeful this was for the continuation of their own race.

Suddenly, the ostrich coverage ended, and the video and data coverage returned to the drone's primary mission. They watched a wandering group of nomads get pink-fried then collapse onto the sandy desert to die quickly. Meanwhile, Drone#1 was finishing up its coverage of the Indian sub-continent as it had already made careful analysis of all the death and destruction previously unleashed over Pakistan, Kashmir, and northern India due to their nuclear war. In order to remediate the contamination and disease still prevalent on the land beneath it, the drone increased the revolutions of its toroid and vacuumed up the high-levels of pulverized ash and dust while simultaneously irradiating the decimated lands below with UV light in order to kill and sterilize the disease organisms still clinging to life while festering within the multitudes of long-dead and rotting corpses. So sophisticated were the drone's analytical abilities that Krawwgh and Klaarongah would receive updated radiological, biological, and environmental survey reports to identify any hazardous areas they might encounter upon landing or exploring. Foremost always was the consideration of how to protect the indigenous, natural flora and fauna, and how to support the return of normal ecological balances.

Inexorably onward, the two drones progressed in their missions until, by the end of the fourth day, they had crisscrossed over each other's flight patterns at least twice and assured the deaths of over nine billion people. Most had experienced the lovely pink and orange hue before their immediate deaths, while many others were rendered unconscious by massive seizures, never knowing what had just happened as the super-potent neuro-toxin took hold. Lastly were the unlucky few who were either incinerated by the weapon beams directly, or those near nuclear weapons and materials-targeted for destruction.

Except for the few thousand primitive people living within the same large grassy-savannahs of central-East Africa as occupied by the selected breed of ostriches, ALL HUMAN LIFE AND CIVILIZATION HAD ENDED! In just over four days, the planetary menace had been exterminated, and the healing of Earth was at hand. This erasure of mankind would not extend to many of its cultural and architectural achievements. Instead, much of the unique art, architecture, and writings of previous cultures had already been vandalized and destroyed by evangelized 'warriors' from conquering tribes bent on the subjugation and erasure of their fallen and 'less worthy' foes. Now, any such cultural treasures discovered would be carefully analyzed and recorded for posterity. It seemed ironic to Klaarongah and Krawwgh that their own culture had likely been catalogued for posterity as well—though in its case for a natural, unavoidable reason: EXTINCTION, not annihilation! Who would be left to learn about it? Perhaps, some other inter-stellar travelers and world explorers eons from now? Klaarongah then wondered to herself what the historians back on Kaarp had written about this admittedly expensive and risky mission. Was it worth it? Only time would tell.

XII. Getting Acquainted!

A couple of hours had passed since the drones last reported census had been performed and tabulated. They reconfirmed that except for the few thousand allowed to exist because of their close proximity to the precious ostriches in central-East Africa, no other humans were left alive. These lucky few were comprised of mostly desperately poor rebel nomads, armed with no more than a few firearms and grenade launchers, ferried about on camels and a couple of jeeps whose wheels would soon grow permanently still, as access to gasoline came to an end. The drones had had seen to it that ALL pollutants and their sources were terminated, including oil refineries and their associated storage tanks.

Barely a month later, both drones had completed all their environmental remediation tasks and Drone#2 had finished collecting and categorizing all the data concerning life on Earth. Having successfully finished all their respective tasks, the two drones no longer served any purpose. They had cleared the way for Klaarongah and Krawwgh to perform their parts of the mission—the annihilation of the few remaining humans, and then mating with the ostriches. Since the drones were such incredibly powerful weapons that had genocidal and planet-altering abilities, they couldn't be left idly by, eventually to be forgotten or left unguarded. No responsible society would run the risk of such dangerous devices falling into the clutches of future beings—whose intentions could never be known. So their destruction was absolutely necessary and part of the mission's plan. One day, at a designated time and predetermined coordinates 500 miles above the surface of the South Pacific, Klaarongah and Krawwgh stood side-by-side, motionless with a respectful awe, staring at the giant viewing screen as the scene unfolded. This time only Drone#2 had to execute the spectacularly dangerous flip. It did so with the same flawless precision as before and then linked up to the underside of Drone#1. In synchronous unison, they accelerated their toroids and ignited their rockets, then hurtled away from Earth. In just under a day, the drones passed the Planets Venus and then Mercury, sending huge data and holographic video streams about both to the life pod before their collision with the sun.

Krawwgh and Klaarongah would spend much time learning all they could from the received data downloaded to the computer aboard the life pod, still hiding behind the asteroid 150 million miles away.

Only a few days later, however, the life pod was now locked in geo-synchronous orbit over the pre-selected coordinates for the landing site on Earth. It was a flat and pre-historic river bed in the Sahel region of southern Ethiopia coincidentally not far from fossil beds that contained some of the oldest fossils of proto-humans, the pre-historic relatives of those creatures they had just all but exterminated. They performed a quick neutron soil-density scan, and then a pulsed sonic test on the landing site to assure its surface was strong enough to support the life pod's weight. Krawwgh reviewed and approved the analysis, re-checked the coordinates, and then softly cawed for Klaarongah to come over and use her dexterous fingers to dial in the landing coordinates and activate the computerized auto-pilot's landing program. It was set to begin final countdown and land exactly two hours from now, giving them ample time to select and performance-check all their excursion gear and equipment, as well as review all the expected social protocol and likely psychological responses of any people they might encounter. They would initially attempt a peaceful, non-confrontational approach to any of the humans and offer them a chance to remain alive and co-exist peacefully. After all, their tiny numbers and lack of technical knowledge or ability no longer posed any threats to the environment or their fellow creatures, so why not give them a second chance? To this plan, they would extend the peaceful offer, but remain acutely aware and able to respond to anything, just in case.

Two hours later, Klaarongah and Krawwgh were safely nestled in their vibration dampening, cocoon hammocks ready for the descent. It would prove to be a pretty bumpy ride as crosswinds buffeted the large vessel. Nonetheless, it made a safe and gentle landing on the pre-historic riverbed, announced by tremendous noise, exhausted air and melted splotches of sand beneath the vertical deceleration rocket's glaring-red exhaust. At Klaarongah's side was a foot-long infrared laser cannon capable of shooting a concentrated, lethal ruby-red beam, or able to emit a wide array of severely painful and invisible heat rays to drive back a crowd or disarm any attackers. They each were girded in an armored vest and encounter-helmet as well. The latter item was a true marvel of technology. Not only could it effectively protect the wearer's head from various kinds of projectiles and lasers, but it also was designed with special visors that could greatly magnify images as well as provide the wearer with a much-increased view field. As great as these two features were, however, they paled in comparison to the helmet's built-in interpreter. Multiple tiny cameras were attached to an equally small, but very powerful computer whose memory banks were already loaded with a huge assortment of drone-observed and interpreted human and animal behaviors. As either of the intrepid star travelers encountered any humans, all the tiny cameras and audio sensors would focus on several areas of the person's body as well as the mouth. Then they would begin imparting observations and their meanings to tiny dancing figures and symbols located in the lower corners of each eye's vision field on the visor. These figures would interpret the spoken language into the dance language of the krrugh. Conversely, many of these same tiny cameras and audio sensors would couple up with a very sensitive net of accelerometers and motion sensors located within the same helmet. These would notice any of Klaarongah's or Krawwgh's movements and interpret them into the human, spoken language—in this case, a dialect of Oromo, an ancient local tongue. Again, all this technology was vitally necessary because of Klaarongah's and Krawwgh's inability to speak.

After landing, they ran a last-minute scan of the ship's on-board sensors to check for any damages or problems that might have occurred. None were reported, so Krawwgh hobbled over to the view screen and switched it on. Off in the distance but rapidly approaching them, he saw a mob of humans lead by a couple of machine-gun-mounted jeeps and rifle-toting men riding big dromedary camels. Much of the crowd was ululating and emitting war whoops as they ran to catch up with the camels and jeeps. Being sure to display no fear or timidity to the approaching mob, Klaarongah immediately lowered the boarding plank and prominently strode her way down its steps to greet the throng. It was at this same instant that Krawwgh flexed his stout, springy ankles and leaped into the air, quickly gaining altitude with a couple of flaps of his huge wings. He began circling higher-taking ample opportunity to cast his huge and ominous shadow over the crowd below as Klaarongah dealt with them directly.

As expected, one of the jeeps emerged from the crowd and drove in a slow, deliberate arc in front of the people before coming to a stop directly in front of Klaarongah. A tall man wearing an all-black head garb and camouflaged military fatigues was standing by a pole-mounted machine-gun in the back of the jeep. He jumped out and strutted imperiously towards Klaarongah, showing no obvious signs of fear, even though she was a gigantic bird much bigger and far more imposing than him. With nothing but peaceful intent and respectful diplomacy on her mind, she graciously bowed as the strange creature approached—all the while frantically scanning the 'little dancers' inside her visor for any insights on the being's behaviors. As he furiously shouted at her, apparently enraged by current events, Klaarongah kept her cool and even offered another respectful curtsy. This was having no effect on soothing his rage nor curb his insults, and she hadn't yet had a chance to even respond. But as his hands began gripping the shoulder-slung Kalashnikov, and a finger moved towards its trigger, she knew what had to be done. Klaarongah reacted with some rage of her own. She thrust her right forelimb into the rebel leader's chest, knocking him to the ground. Then, she stomped a huge talon down on him. Under her crushing weight, he was helpless, but he still kept screaming insults and accusations at her, while the crowd grew irate. So with grim resolution and indignant rage, she raised her huge beak skyward, and then arced it down on his mid-section, nearly cutting him in two. She beak-gouged him two more times, killing him in the process. The now terrified group of onlookers gasped in horror. Then, in a savage display of disregard for the man and his demeanor as well as to establish her physical dominance over them all, she pulled out a big length of his coiled intestines and ferociously chomped down on it, spraying blood and shit all over the hysterical crowd. Some people fainted. Others turned quickly and ran away, screaming. Remembering her infrared cannon, Klaarongah grasped it and stood ready, just in case someone in the fleeing throng had a sudden change of mind.

It turned out that someone still harbored plenty of unabated rage against her. Flying nearly a mile above, Krawwgh was watching it all unfold and missed nothing. His focus was drawn towards a single machine-gun-mounted jeep at the rear of the crowd that was now approaching Klaarongah in an unmistakable zig-zag attack pattern. Krawwgh studied the jeep's pattern of motion through his encounter helmet's visor, and with his astounding natural skill, enhanced by the equipment, he was able to mentally plot out an angle of attack on the approaching jeep. Taking in a huge gulp of air, Krawwgh began his dive-bomb run. When he was just about to collide with the vehicle's left rear tire-well, he was a 160-pound wrecking ball of air-inflated muscle, diving chest first into the oncoming vehicle at well over 100 miles per hour. The force of the impact was just short of being explosive as Krawwgh's muscle-cushioned breast slammed so hard into the left rear-wheel that it bent the axle inward, instantly stopping the jeep's forward trajectory and making it pirouette halfway around, while tossing all three passengers out of it. Two of the passengers were thrown head-first into a local sand dune, breaking their necks and killing them instantly. The third lay dying not far from the jeep with his back broken in half, and moaning in rapidly numbing agony. Krawwgh was also nearby, but unscathed. This was his usual method for hunting large prey, and the huge gulp of air he took before the dive, protected his internal organs from injury by acting like a gas-filled shock absorber, expelling the air upon impact. Now, he investigated the scene. He first noticed the two dead bodies lying lifelessly still, with their heads buried in the small, sand dune nearby. Then, he heard the soft, low moan of the third man with the severed spine. He assessed the poor man's condition and knew nothing could be done for him. Then, he remembered that all three of them were trying to slaughter Klaarongah. So he grabbed the man's head between his monstrous talons and promptly, twisted it off. Deciding that he should display his unity with Klaarongah and her zero-tolerance for human-sponsored violence, he grabbed the headless corpse, flew back over the retreating crowd, and dropped it down in their midst. More screaming and fainting ensued, but these folks were quickly scooped up by the others, as they all hastened away from the newly arrived visitors.

After meeting up at the life pod's boarding ramp, they 'dance-discussed' the recent events of their first-ever direct encounter with humans. Klaarongah was absolutely astonished at just how arrogant, irrational, and threatening the approaching leader behaved. No matter how offended he was by their presence, now among them, the potentate should have been fearful, polite, and diplomatic, as he surely knew that Klaarongah and Krawwgh were the beings who oversaw the destruction of all humanity. He should have been humble, while realizing his and his tribe's great fortune on having been spared. Clearly, humans weren't rational! Klaarongah and Krawwgh immediately switched topics and discussed methods they might use to control or tone down the violence whenever they next encountered them. Dejected, they both realized that they could not allow anything or anyone to stand in the way of the successful completion of their mission, even if it meant the absolute annihilation of all humans—every last one.

XIII. Remediation and 'Romance' Ahead

A week had passed since their first direct contact with humans. When they weren't busy launching swarms of insect-size water and soil sampling drones to analyze nearby estuaries, Klaarongah and Krawwgh reviewed all the data collected by the krrugh scientists during their long, unconscious, interstellar flight. This was done in order to better understand and respond to these roving bands of survivors. As they continued to scan the data banks, they learned much about these people—Ethiopians and Somalis—regarding how tough and resourceful they had become, while surviving continual droughts, sandstorms, famines, and diseases—as well as one another's ceaseless battles over tribal commands and religious identity and authority. This filled them both with despair, because the tell-tale signs of religiously inspired intolerance meant that most of these beings would never be able to peacefully co-exist, let alone accept Klaarongah and Krawwgh as anything other than two demons thrust down from the skies and into their midst. Most likely the humans would avoid any further contact until they had gathered enough people to overwhelm them in some savage, big battle.

Neither Klaarongah nor Krawwgh were frightened by this realization, but they were concerned that it might interfere with their mission objectives of continued environmental remediation, species conservation, and attempted breeding. This could not be allowed. They would have to protect against any attempts on their lives by humans or large predators, and guard against damage and theft to their vessel and equipment. The fate of these remaining tribes was in their own hands now, in how they intended to deal with the continued presence of their new and permanent neighbors from the stars.

While they continued all their environmental remediation duties, they also began determining the best way to mate with the ostriches. After releasing a swarm of species specific, tiny blood-sampling drones, they analyzed many collected samples and were quite pleased to confirm just how similar the ostriches' genes were with their own. Still, there were profound differences. The two biggest challenges they faced were: locating the specific set of genes within the ostriches' complex molecular coil of DNA that coded for skull and brain development and replacing them with the engineered genes on an artificial chromatid to correctly pattern up with the ostriches' inferior alleles. If successful, this would 'encephalize' the ovum and make the hybrid infant intelligent, like all Krrugh. By making the hybrids intelligent, the krrugh reasoned that this would greatly increase their chances for survival in this new world, and better able to manage and protect it.

Aside from all this theoretical and laboratory-based science, they both knew that in order to ensure a successful fertilization, they would have to engage in a lot of field research. By practicing and perfecting all the ostriches' courting and mating rituals, while also sampling and duplicating their natural scents, they could put the skittish animals at ease, and make the experience as natural as possible. Since both Klaarongah's and Krawwgh's biological clocks and rhythms were adjusting beautifully to their new world's much longer days and nights, they were hurtling through all the mission goals and support research. This left them at least a little time for recreation. Between their intense sessions in any number of the life pod's labs', they would engage in spontaneous mock ambushes and battles where Krawwgh would gently wing-beat Klaarongah and goose her rear with his pointy beak. While other times, she would sneak up, pin him to the ground, and delightfully scratch his back or belly with her monstrous down-thrusting over-beak. These playful bouts often ended in loving trysts, which they knew would soon curtail once the breeding trials with the ostriches began. Then, they would have to store up all their focused energy and precious reserves of bodily fluids, for this vital part of the mission.

With each passing day, more data was pouring in from all the environmental analyses and endangered-species inventories, and the news was quite good. The Earth's natural ecological cycles were returning to normal pre-human levels, and all the identified animals and plants doomed to a man-made extinction were now rebounding instead. Together they studied and learned all they could about life on Earth. To them, all the life on this beautiful world further confirmed the same patterns seen on all the other worlds their race had explored so far. The evolution of life ALWAYS AND ULTIMATELY being reduced to the non-random survival of randomly varying replicators, in other words, GENES being subjected to the immensely selective but totally thoughtless processes of Natural Selection.

One day, a little more than a month after they had landed on Earth, and had that violent confrontation with humans, Klaarongah and Krawwgh went out into the savannah to observe the ostriches, together. They decided that equipment should be kept to a minimum when away from the vessel, in order to reduce the risks of something falling into the wrong hands. When they left the life pod that morning, after turning on its lethal electro-magnetic security shield and optically scrambling camouflage unit, they ventured out into the wilderness, unencumbered by technology and determined to rely on nothing but their natural abilities. At first, Klaarongah enjoyed a great and lengthy gallop that stretched out her huge muscles. Then, she accelerated into a sprint as her talons sprung up from the dusty clumps of sand and grass with each huge stride. Meanwhile, Krawwgh had vaulted into the air the moment he was outside the ship's hatch and was flapping his colossal wings as he alternatingly stretched and contracted his massive breast and shoulder muscles while climbing skyward. Then, he worked a dizzying array of smaller muscles and tendons as he executed sharp turns and spins before circling back towards Klaarongah in a pattern of lazy eights. In just under half an hour, they had covered nearly 40 miles with no signs of either ostriches or humans. The absence of people concerned them, because they thought that Krawwgh would have spotted an empty campsite or some abandoned jeeps. This lack of jeeps must have meant that some of the tribes still had small caches of fuel hidden somewhere, because the drones would have easily detected and destroyed any large reserves. Their concern was interrupted when Krawwgh suddenly spotted something off to his left. It was a large clutch of ostriches sprinting away from them some 20 miles distant. Krawwgh let out a low, long honk, letting Klaarongah know that he had spotted their 'prey' and to get ready! Knowing exactly what to expect, Klaarongah broke out into a sprint again, but this time, with her forelimbs and neck lowered out in front of her, while Krawwgh swooped down on her with his strong talons extended. As he glided toward her from above and behind, he slowed his air speed to match hers by furiously pumping his fully unfurled 25-foot wingspan, and he then grabbed her by her thickly feathered flanks, as he mashed his huge chest onto her broad back. With powerful down-beats, he pumped his wings again and completely lifted his 500 pound companion from the ground, rising 15 feet into the air and gliding several yards before they touched back down on Klaarongah's flexed talons, ready to vault again for another short glide. They repeated this display of tremendous power, coordination, and cooperation while accelerating to nearly a 100 miles per hour, rapidly gaining on the pack of ostriches, still far in the distance. This highly efficient form of travel, called 'hop-gliding,' greatly increased their speed and range while considerably reducing their individual exertions.

Within minutes, they were close to the ostriches, busy grazing on seeds, insects, and pebbles. As they cautiously approached so as not to spook the creatures, notorious for their keen eyesight, Klaarongah and Krawwgh silently decoupled and assumed low-profile squats behind a nearby bush. It was early April, right near the beginning of their mating season, and a perfect time for them to study ostrich courtship rituals.

Ostriches traveled in packs, and males had to put on elaborate displays for female attention and then battle for the chance to mate. These female sexual selection pressures drove males to become significantly bigger, in order to be worthwhile combatants for consideration as viable mates. Three tall males were among the pack of thirty-some members, which was comprised of at least a few breeding-age females and numerous adolescents and chicks. The feathers started to fly as two of the males quickly got into it! They nipped and pecked at one another, then began furiously flapping their large wings while viciously kicking their dagger-sharp talons. Their powerful legs delivered some truly injurious and possibly dangerous kicks, but luckily, the conflict ended quite suddenly, with the loser jogging off in defeat. Being noticeably smaller than the victor, the other male chickened out, and sauntered off as well. At this point, Krawwgh paid extra-close attention to the victor's courtship rituals.

First, the male began strutting in front and all around a couple of the females. His red throat became a sudden undulating pipe of vocal activity as he began his chorus of very deep and resonant throat booms. On and on this went. He also began flexing his wings downward and pecking at the ground. Then, he would interrupt these activities by running around the females, while simultaneously rotating his head and long sinewy neck from the base of his big body. This strange set of displays eventually did the trick, and soon one of the females was squatting on the ground, displaying her interest. Klaarongah had been studying the activities as well, knowing that she would have to act as passively receptive as the female in order to successfully attempt mating and hopeful conception. They continued their clandestine field observations until nightfall. Then, they re-united for a long and rapid hop-glide back to the life pod.

They repeated this pattern for the next several days, after the completion of their daily shipboard checks and maintenance duties, as well as the continual environmental monitoring and checking for any incoming signals from home—just now reaching them from across the stellar void. They spent most of their mornings in the bio-lab, analyzing and tinkering with their engineered sperms and eggs, trying to assure successful fertilization and the transference of many of their krrugh traits—especially superior brain development. Then, they enjoyed a quick meal, dining on the rapidly dwindling supply of frozen carcasses from the giant walk-in freezer. After the meal, they went to the engineering lab to work on a more ostrich-like costume for Krawwgh. Since Klaarongah's body was much more like their own, the males probably wouldn't be spooked by her otherwise, obvious differences in size and head-shape. Krawwgh looked and moved nothing like them however, so he would need a mechanized disguise to convince them that he was one of them, a powerful male capable of fierce rivalry and worthy of mating. They tended to this task as well for a couple of late mornings, before embarking on their daily afternoon journey to observe the birds.

A few days later, after carefully processing their respective sex cells, and then applying them to their sex organs, they both took off in the general direction of some of the earlier ostrich gatherings. Because they were carrying equipment and materials necessary for the upcoming first-ever tryst with the ostriches, and because in the several days they had previously ventured out to study them, they had never encountered any humans along the way, they both felt safe leaving their encounter helmets, body armor, and infrared cannons behind. This was unfortunate, because as they raced across the desert, seeking out their rendezvous, they were being watched by hidden and vengeful eyes!

Hiding in a thicket of tall savannah grass, sat two of the 50-caliber machine-gun-mounted jeeps, with another black head-scarfed potentate watching their every move, through his antique Zeiss-brand binoculars. He noticed their direction towards the grazing ostriches in the distance and schemed that he'd sit, watch and wait for the right time to pounce. If only Krawwgh or Klaarongah had been wearing one of their encounter helmets, they would have immediately detected the jeep's exhaust plumes and engine heat in the infrared spectrum of the helmet's visor, and thus, forewarned. They weren't however, and since their task ahead required so much concentration and preparation from them both, they missed an otherwise, easy clue.

As they hid themselves behind another thicket of tall grass, Klaarongah watched the birds as she doused herself with female ostrich scent and mentally rehearsed all her expected movements and behaviors. She also remembered to walk in a somewhat crouched position, so that she wouldn't confuse or freak out any of the available males by her considerably larger size. Before she set out to entice an ostrich mate, she had to help Krawwgh get into his mechanized costume, adorned as it was, with a tiny, big-eyed head attached to a long rubbery and gyrating neck which nestled on top of his own, and his stilted artificial legs. Klaarongah silently reared her big head up and then quickly dipped her beak in a series of 'laughs' at the comical site of her mate, who promptly spun around on one stilt, then the other, to join her in acknowledging the comical situation. However, fooling the ostriches was no laughing matter, and as Klaarongah snuck out of the grass to begin her routine, hoping to garner some male attention in the process, Krawwgh finished his mental rehearsal and then doused himself with male ostrich scent, before erupting on the group.

Sure enough, a big male took notice of Klaarongah and started his neck swivels, throat boom sonata, and ground pecks. Hoping to rile him up a little, and get him fully aroused for best chances of conception, Klaarongah made him work for it, before she submitted. Pushing from her mind the natural revulsion and humiliation she felt, while squatting down before the feral and small-minded creature, she did everything she could to keep from looking rearward as he finished his business. During the hours before nightfall, she would have to endure several more sessions with the beast, all the while hoping for a successful conception in order to propagate krrugh traits into the future on this new world. All revulsion aside, she would endure whatever it took, and so too, would her mate.

Krawwgh had slipped out of the bushes only moments after Klaarongah, and his task would be a trifle more difficult. First, while he was hindered by the awkward costume he would be immediately challenged by the alpha male. Being a much more powerful creature, and a natural top of the food chain predator, he'd have to withhold much of his strength, and purposely dull his reflexes, so as not to kill or maim any of the males, while arranging to lose a convincing battle. Lastly, he'd have to patiently wait till the alpha male was done, in order to slip in behind him and re-copulate the female with 'his own special blend.' As the big male approached, he articulated and gestured his artificial neck and mock beak, and then scraped the ground with his stilted false-talon to engage in battle. The ostrich was upon him immediately, pecking and wing-beating him while also delivering powerful front kicks. Krawwgh patiently endured the assault, only returning volley with a half-hearted wing bash to his temporarily stunned, but determined opponent. After several minutes of convincing combat, Krawwgh retreated to the periphery of the group—just like all vanquished males did. Suffering only mild scratches and bruises from the altercation, Krawwgh rested comfortably, fondly recalling all the mock battles and talon grappling sessions of his long ago and far away youth on Planet Kaarp. The big male that had just bested him, was back, pestering poor Klaarongah, for another round of bliss. Since he was well distracted, Krawwgh took the opportunity to sneak up behind one of the females and charm her into position. Vigorously rubbing his erection against her cloaca, she squatted and then, just before penetration, he pressed one of the small syringes attached to his penis. This one would vacuum out the semen of the previous encounter, and then he'd press on another to inject his own, engineered seed. He finished just in time, as the alpha male was coming after him again. Like any dominated male, he ran away and headed back into the thicket of tall grass. Soon, nightfall would approach and reprieve them both, from this humiliating duty.

From his perch standing by the machine-gunner, in the back of the jeep, that other black-scarfed and camouflage-dressed potentate smirked in disgust, upon witnessing the mating spectacle before him. "These mighty war birds fuck ostriches." He obscenely whispered to his sniggering subordinates, in their Oromo tongue. He couldn't believe he was seeing the very same creature that sliced his own big brother in half, now squatting submissively before a lowly, stupid ostrich. She would soon be squatting before him, DEAD! He whispered orders for his drivers and machine-gunners to remain in the jeeps, while the rest of them would sneak into the thicket of tall grass near the ostriches, and their prey.

They were in the thicket of tall grass for only a moment, with Klaarongah helping Krawwgh out of his ostrich costume, when it started. Six men left the two jeeps, and headed into the thicket. They formed a large circle around the two of them, and immediately started shooting, as they closed in on the unsuspecting duo. Klaarongah was struck twice in her side, while a bullet glanced off Krawwgh's thick skull, only grazing him. Despite the ambush, both of them were still quite capable of defending themselves, as the marauders would soon discover. Just after a muzzle-blast betrayed its shooter's hidden position in the dense grass, Klaarongah coiled her massive neck and suddenly extended her huge beak at the barrel flame last seen and struck the assassin right in the head, killing him. Meanwhile, Krawwgh had managed to knock another shooter off his feet with a swipe of his wing. He then planted a talon on his ribcage, and crushed his sternum. Seething with rage, he bellowed a deep resonant honk to check on his mate, who promptly snorted a blast from her nostrils, signaling she was OK and was busy killing.

Just then, they both heard one of the jeeps starting in the clearing nearby. Krawwgh sprang from the thicket, and, beating his giant wings as fast as he could, hurtled skyward, until he was at least a half mile up. From this lofty height, he swiveled his big head around until he caught sight of the billowing dust trail, following the fleeing jeep. He locked onto the vehicle and calculated his plan of attack. Flying even higher, while moving a lot faster than the jeep, he got way ahead of it, and then turned to face the approaching vehicle. Krawwgh drew in another huge breath and began his dive run. Since he was swooping down on them in the dark, like an incoming cruise missile at over a 100 miles per hour, they never knew what hit them. He smashed, breast-first, into the oncoming jeep's windshield, instantly decapitating both, the driver and black-scarfed commander. His momentum carried him into the machine-gun-mount and gunner. All three men were killed instantly, and the driverless jeep careened into a small dune and flipped on its side, spilling the last of its precious fuel on the thirsty sand. Clearing his head from the effects of the colossal collision, Krawwgh made quick note of the bodies' locations, then vaulted back up in the sky to glide back to his companion, whom he had left with her own battle back at that thicket of tall grass. Constantly scanning over the ground below, he soon saw her, sitting and resting in the grassy covering. She noticed him and gently cawed out. A minute later, he was by her side and checking her wounds. She had killed two assassins, while the third drove off, fleeing for his life. The wounds she suffered were deep and bleeding heavily. Thinking quickly, Krawwgh plucked out a couple clumps of his belly feathers and gave them to her to roll up and insert into the circular wounds, effectively stopping the bleeding. He would fly back to the life pod and retrieve an emergency supply kit, and some of their weapons and armor. First, he waddled over to the assassins' guns and laid them at her side, confident that Klaarongah could defend herself from any returning marauders or curious predators that might, happen by. Next, he lay on his side to chomp-off a bunch of blades of the tall grass, and dragged them over to Klaarongah. Then, he covered his badly wounded mate with the foliage, camouflaging and keep her warm until his return. Krawwgh gently enfolded Klaarongah in his wings and gave her a loving eye-touch kiss, then sprung from the thicket and began flying as fast as he could back to the life pod, nearly a hundred miles away. Klaarongah watched her loving mate hurtle away, trusting completely in him, and his hasty return. Any doubts she had were with herself, and her continued ability to stay alert and fight off any intruders. She quickly calmed her worries though, as she remembered how tough, brave, and resourceful she was only moments ago, when she and her mate had repelled and survived a deadly ambush, and then killed off all but one, assassin.

Krawwgh flew at nearly 120 miles per hour—as fast as he could go in a straight line—back to the life pod. As a natural stellar navigator, he had familiarized himself with Earth's night sky and used the stars to adjust the flight, and keep it as straight and short as possible. Three quarters of an hour later, and he knew he was in the immediate vicinity of the vessel. He landed in the area and began his elaborate dance. One of its onboard security cameras witnessed the dance and deactivated the cloaking and shock-security devices. Wasting no time, he scurried up the ramp and grabbed a large, black and ultra-tough, poly bag and collected two helmets, a set of his and her body armor, and two one-foot-long infrared cannons. Next, he waddled over to the medical/surgical lab and retrieved an emergency medical kit. He checked its contents to assure it had all the necessary equipment and supplies for performing surgery in the field. Then, he got a large collapsible water-tote bottle. He reached into the poly bag to retrieve and put on his form-fitted body armor and an encounter helmet. He had everything needed and was now securely protected and pre-warned. He left the ship, reactivated its electric shock security and invisibility devices, and took flight back to his endangered mate.

Since he was now wearing gear and carrying a big bag full of supplies and weapons, his air speed was considerably slower, but he still managed a Herculean 70 miles per hour, carrying over half his body weight. Of course, this would lengthen his return time to Klaarongah by a half-hour or more, but was unavoidable. He knew that she knew he would get back to her as soon as possible.

Conserving her energy while remaining as still and quiet as possible, Klaarongah heard something rustling just south of her position. Then, she heard the unmistakable cackling howls and alerted growls of a pack of hyenas. Thinking quickly, she stretched out a leg and slowly, silently pushed out one of the assassin's corpses from the thicket, while she raised and aimed one of the Kalashnikovs, just in case. As she sat there, silent and motionless, one of the hyenas discovered the corpse, and let out a howl. It then chomped on a leg. Klaarongah feathered the trigger, ready to slaughter the beast and its approaching companions at any second. She was greatly relieved when she noticed the hyenas were pre-occupied with their new-found feast and were totally unaware of her. They growled and snapped their powerful jaws at one another in hungry frustration, while struggling and tearing at the corpse's clothing. Klaarongah felt a pain surge through her, while her vision began to blur. Then, she suffered a spell of dizziness. This filled her with terror and adrenaline, as she struggled to remain alert and ready. But how much longer could she hold out in this weakened state? The hyenas had already chewed through and shredded the pants of the corpse, and then flipped it over to chomp on the savory fat and muscles of its butt and thighs. Her pain and dizziness increased, while she struggled to remain alert. She knew Krawwgh would return shortly and either run-off or kill these creatures, so she'd have to hang tough.

Just then, she was startled to full attention when something really big came crashing out of the dark. It was a male lion, and as Klaarongah strained to see more of his features and interpret his intensions, she saw the chewed-off ear and gouged-out eye socket, clearly marking him as an old rogue, long-vanquished from his pride by a younger male. No doubt, starving and desperate, he was there to steal the hyena's find. As one of the hyenas assaulted his blind side, the lion quickly spun around and smashed it with its left forepaw, killing it instantly. Another hyena crouched in behind him and bit one of his haunches, causing him to roar in pain, then pivot and swipe with the other massive paw, just barely missing. The lion now stood over the half-eaten corpse, roaring his threats as the two remaining hyenas slowly, reluctantly retreated into the night, growling, whining, and cackling in anger and defeat.

As Klaarongah sat there watching the savage battle unfold, her remaining strength and alertness were ebbing fast. Her wounds had started bleeding again in earnest. Struggling to remain conscious, she stared at the big cat as he did what nature intended—gnaw on his stolen prize. A strange sense of tranquility blanketed her, as she realized she was going to pass out and likely die in this savage, but entirely natural, setting. It was an otherwise peaceful, beautiful starlit night with that big, bright, silvery moon shining high in the sky. As her last thoughts turned to her loving companion, she continued staring at that awesome moon, imagining it was his wide-eyed, big-beaked face, coming to snuggle her.

She awoke to some moisture sprinkling on her talon. Thinking it was a very light rain starting, her eyes refocused, and then she realized it was drool from that rogue lion. It must have smelled all the blood around her and was poking its big head into the thicket to investigate when ALL of a sudden, he expelled a huge blood-spewing roar and promptly keeled over on his side, dead! Krawwgh had seen the lion approaching the thicket from up high, and knew that in her severely weakened state she was in mortal danger. Holding his bag of tricks, he reached in and retrieved one of the infrared laser cannons. Then, he set it on high-focused, maximum energy. He took careful aim at the big lion's broad flank and fired, instantly searing a huge, cauterized hole completely through the animal's body. Still tightly clasping the big black bag, laser-cannon, and collapsed water bottle, Krawwgh circled over his lover and slowly descended down into the tall grass thicket next to her. Krawwgh pulled out the emergency medical kit and opened one of the pill pouches. Cushioning Klaarongah's head on one of his wing-tips, he gently lifted it and placed an anesthetic pill in her beak while lightly stroking her throat with his other wing, causing her to swallow, involuntarily. The pill, plus her weakened state, rendered her completely unconscious in seconds. Krawwgh pulled out the infrared heater, gamma-source sterilizer, surgical instruments, sterile wound gauze pads, and anti-microbial ointments, then went to work. He applied a chemical sterilizer to his beak and talons then put the surgical coring knife and retractor pliers in the small, radioisotope-powered sterilizer box, where the equipment's surfaces would be bathed in an intense field of gamma rays, which quickly killed all microbial life. While waiting for the instrument sterilizer to finish, he sat on his rump and picked up a large tube of the anti-microbial ointment. The cap popped open with a slight squeeze of his mighty talon, and he liberally coated the two wound holes and surrounding skin.

With his sterilized beak, he pulled out the wadded belly feathers that she had stuffed into the wounds earlier. Since she was very weak from all her blood loss, he needed to hurry with the surgery so that he could administer the hemo-equivalence drug that would kick her red marrow and spleen into over drive, reproducing red blood cells and plasma. He took the sterilized coring knife into his beak and carved into first, one wound, and then the other. She was hemorrhaging now, so he had to work fast. Next, he took the retractor pliers in his beak and reached into both of the wounds, feeling around each time for the bullet's casing and then clamping the casing with the pliers to retrieve each bullet. Now, he was finally able to squirt the tube of anti-microbial ointment into the bleeding wounds. This would also help constrict blood flow, while he packed each deep wound with a tampon made of sterilized, bio-absorbable wound gauze. Lastly, he would cauterize the two wounds with the medical infrared heater, and administer the hemo-equivalence drug to replenish her significant blood loss.

He soon finished with the surgery and quickly cleaned up her wounds. Her vital signs were rapidly increasing, which indicated that her blood levels were normalizing, and she was recovering. He bent down over her to soothingly rub her head and parched throat. He gave her another loving eye-kiss as she comfortably snoozed. After all she'd been through, he hated leaving her yet again, but knew he must in order to fetch them water and then get himself something to eat, because he was now so hungry that his own strength was beginning to ebb. First, though, he would leave her clean, warm, and as safe and secure as possible.

Since it was still dark, he decided to leave the big lion's carcass right where it lay, reasoning that at least any predators that saw it from a distance might think he was just sleeping by the thicket, and not to be provoked. Then, he noticed the dead hyena, apparently the result of an earlier confrontation with the rogue. He dragged it into the thicket and placed it close by Klaarongah, so that she could begin dining on it—if she wanted. The carcass was only meaty enough to suffice her current needs. Since her wounds were externally healed, there was no risk of infection and this time he covered Klaarongah and the carcass with the foliage. All he had to do now was to find a nearby stream and fill the collapsible poly bottle with some precious, cool water. First, though, he badly needed a nibble of something to tide him over. Having survived an ambush with his loving mate, and now aware of humanity's disregard for peace, Krawwgh felt no remorse or hesitation in consuming them. Despite their evolved minds, humans were spectacularly wasteful and warlike, and gave little care about their world or fellow species. They were nothing like the krrugh! He remembered the location of the three corpses he left behind, after his dive bomb assault on the fleeing cowards.

In less than five minutes, he landed next to their bodies, which had been picked over by vultures. The headless potentate had the most flesh left, so as he contemplated human anatomy for a brief couple of seconds, he then waddled over to the body's right side. Krawwgh flicked the arm out of the way and aligned himself at the corpse's rib cage. Probing amid the ribs with his pointy beak, he found the sweet spot and then coiled his powerful neck back and then thrusted his beak between the lower two ribs in a savage, stabbing strike. He was instantly rewarded with a gush of rich deep-red blood, and as it flowed, he continued reaming deeper into the corpse's liver, tearing out and gobbling up big chunks of the calorically rich organ tissue. Soon, he felt rejuvenated and stopped, as he had to find water and return to Klaarongah. It had been a merciful thing that this modern day 'Prometheus' was already dead, and therefore, oblivious to what this mighty eagle—sent from the Gods—had done to him. He quickly grabbed up the bottle and launched himself skyward, climbing ever higher, in search of water. Since he still had his encounter helmet on, he switched over to the infrared night vision, and as he scanned the glowingly hot sands below, it wasn't too long before he noticed some darkened areas, signaling a cool, sandy spring underneath. He circled down and landed in the spring, enjoying the cool mud on his talons as he clawed it away. Then, he dropped a sanitation tablet in the poly bottle, before dipping it into the stream.

In the few minutes since Krawwgh left for water, Klaarongah awoke from her anesthetized state, terrified. The last thing she remembered was that big drooling lion about to pounce on her. Coming too, she quickly surveyed her surroundings and her fear subsided, as she realized Krawwgh had already returned in the nick of time and ruby-fried the lion.

He then performed surgery on her. Still covered in camouflage foliage, while hidden in the thicket she judged that it was safe to take a quick peek out through the thick blades. Sure enough, the lion carcass was only two feet from her, laying where it died, and with a huge hole burned clean through its body. She exhaled a snort of relief and then yawned. She straightened her long, stiff legs and felt her talons bump into something next to her, also hidden under the foliage. She brushed the grassy coverage aside, and marveled at the hyena carcass Krawwgh had so thoughtfully placed beside her. Despite a painful twinge in the side, Klaarongah managed to bend down and chomp a big chunk out, of the dead animal's belly, and relished the blood-soaked, slimy rope of the hyena's intestines sliding down her long, parched throat. She was starving but even thirstier, and let out a joyous series of caws, as she saw Krawwgh approaching.

Soon, they were together, and Krawwgh nuzzled and eye-kissed his rebounding patient, then inserted the plastic hose tubes in both their throats, as Klaarongah gently lifted and tilted the bottle, to start the flow. After a very delightful and relieving drink, they started in on the rest of the scrawny hyena. Together, they finished out the cold desert evening, eating and celebrating their still being alive, while humbled by their serious breach from mission-trained safety and security protocols, no matter how inconvenient. For this reason, after they finished devouring the hyena, and slaking their thirsts with the soothing, cool water, Krawwgh slept with his sensory-enhancing encounter helmet on while Klaarongah slept at his side, her sleepy head resting on his meal-swollen belly. Together, hiding in the thicket, with at least one of them wearing a helmet, they'd be safe and sleep until sunrise.

As soon as the rays of sunshine bolted over the horizon, Krawwgh awoke, and was very pleased to see his lover still comfortably snoozing—no doubt, exhausted from the previous evening's traumas. So as not to awaken her, he slowly slid out from beneath her massive head, and while gently holding it aloft, reached a talon out to the delightfully smelly hyena remnant, and muscled it over for her weary head, to rest upon. If Klaarongah woke before his return, she would have something to hold her over. He then reached into the medical kit, retrieved a scanner and performed a quick, silent, and non-invasive medical scan on Klaarongah. Paying extra-close attention to the two bullet wounds and the surgical materials, he was pleased to see normal blood flow and no signs of infection. The special bio-absorptive gauze was nearly gone as well. Fondly gazing down on her, he didn't want her to awaken from badly needed rest, so he skipped giving her a kiss and hug. Krawwgh pulled out the other encounter helmet and set the multi-sensor scanners on ALARM. That way, if the sensors picked up on anything bigger than a rat, the helmet would immediately warn Klaarongah. Since he had already placed an armed and activated infrared laser cannon by her side, she'd be ready to repel or kill within a second. And when Klaarongah put her helmet on, she would be in immediate contact with Krawwgh. Confident that she was as safe as she could be—given their rustic conditions—he vaulted into the sky with a laser-cannon, water bottle, and sanitizer tablets, in tow.

He returned to the same coordinates where he found the spring the previous night, and after placing another sanitizing tablet in the bottle, he started filling it up again with the mercifully cool, subterranean bounty. Then, he noticed something in the distance. Something wonderful! Partway down the steep face of a nearby, sky-scraping bluff, was a big, mottle-colored ram, with prominent, straight horns. He had probably climbed down from his usual, loftier elevations, because he felt safe from any lions or hyenas, wearily trying to chase him down in the rapidly climbing temps' of the rising morning sun. As Krawwgh sat there, filling the water bottle, he admired the magnificent beast. It was at peace, chewing some prickly scrub, yet vigilantly scanning its surroundings with its keen vision, while on a high perch of the near vertical cliff. It was unlikely that any creature would be able to climb up and attack, as the ram was more than mighty enough to put up a tough, head-butting battle on the treacherous slope, while also fast and agile enough to scale up to safety in the clouds.

However, he wasn't the only creature at that scenic location that could fight from above. Still fetching water, Krawwgh thought about the ram and what an excellent specimen he was. He loathed the very idea of killing such a fine stud and likely breeder of many healthy offspring, but his ample-size and close proximity made him too good an opportunity to pass up for feeding themselves well, during their arduous journey, back to the life pod. Since the big ram was on such a steep slope, Krawwgh couldn't risk a dive bombing attack and thus, incurring almost certain injury. But the fact that the creature had large, sturdy, and straight horns offered him another way to possibly bring down this prey. He could have descended from the cloud cover and ruby-fried it, as he had done to the lion last night, but knew the powerful laser would incinerate much of the ram's vitally nutritious meat, and it was a cowardly way to hunt such a worthy prey. So instead, he decided to fly towards the top of the cloud-covered bluff, then climb down the steep face until he was in range for attack.

Krawwgh quickly scooped out enough sand to bury and insulate the cool water from the hot sun, and any curious scavengers. Then, he hid the laser-cannon beneath some nearby scrub bushes. Finally, he leaped skyward and circled overhead. He planned to appear as nothing more than a big vulture, and not worthy of the mighty ram's concern, as it continued munching the scraggly plants on the bluff's steep face. Once Krawwgh had reached the cloud-covered peak, he began a series of mini-hops to quickly scale down the bluff's steep face and encounter the ram. When he reached the same narrow ledge, the ram became startled and charged at Krawwgh. At just the right instant, Krawwgh made a small leap and clasped the ram's horns with his monstrously strong talons and then quickly extended a wing to push off the ledge. Ass over appetite, they tumbled down the cliff's face together, with Krawwgh never easing his incredible grip on the ram's horns. He tucked his big beak onto his muscle-padded chest, and rolled with the tumble, minimizing his risk for serious injury. Just as he sensed they were nearing the bottom of their spill, Krawwgh extended a wing and brutally wrenched the ram's horns over towards the bluff's face, while its big body was still rotating in the opposite direction. This promptly snapped the ram's neck in two. The crack echoed like a gunshot across the desiccated valley! Mercifully, he clamped the limp and broken neck in his mighty beak, and bit off the head. As he unfurled and flexed his wings, and then stretched his talons, he knew he was fine—and lucky to have experienced such an encounter, unscathed. Krawwgh marveled at the ram's head, and reflected on what a worthy opponent it was, and how fortunate Klaarongah and he would be, because of the sustenance its death provided them.

Krawwgh knew his next adventure would be carrying the big carcass back to the thicket. Since he couldn't carry the water and the carcass at the same time, he'd have to make two trips. He respectfully mounted the big skull on a spire of rock nearby, and then dragged the heavy carcass down the last few yards of the bluff's face, until he reached a flat and level clearing. As he sat there resting up for his flight, he noticed a couple of large, pointy ears peaking out above some small boulders in the distance. Then, he heard some whining yelps and growls. It was a mother fox and a couple of her cubs, coming to check on all the earlier commotion, and Krawwgh couldn't help but be touched by how adorable and pathetic they were, so he bit-off a meaty foreleg and left it for them.

Then, he grabbed the beast in his talons and began a small, violent dust storm, as he pumped his huge wings as hard as he could and slowly rose, into the sky.

Because of the size of his trophy kill, he was flying slow, low, and unarmed. He'd had to leave the laser-cannon hidden near the buried water bottle. He knew exactly where they were, however, and would fly in a beeline back to retrieve them both. He had been away from Klaarongah for over an hour and needed to get back to her. With all the strength and stamina he could muster, he flew without stopping, the 30-mile course, until he was back in the thicket, proudly laying the slain beast before his wounded fellow warrior and lover. Now, they could feast and rest before undertaking their long journey back home. First, however, he'd have to return and fetch the water and cannon. After a couple of minutes rest, Krawwgh tore out a small chunk of their prize, swallowed it whole, and bolted back into the blue to finish his errand. The rest of the scorching-hot day, they spent together while studying the clutch of ostriches that had returned from the previous day's gathering. Then they leisurely dined on some of their kill, and drank the cool water. As they sat there in the shade of the tall grass thicket, peering out over the big, beautiful birds, they both wondered whether or not all their amorous efforts of the previous day had had any success kindling life, in those big bellies. Klaarongah looked down and gently rubbed hers, and wondered about any life, within. They were too exhausted and banged-up to attempt any further mating for now, so they decided to rest, recuperate, and later, return.

As the sun set, they both donned their body armor and helmets, then corralled all their gear and garbage. Klaarongah pulled the remains of the hyena carcass out into the adjacent clearing, for any nearby scavengers, then slung one of the infrared laser cannons and the five-gallon water bottle over her neck. In addition to the risk of reinjuring the recovering bullet wounds, they had too much equipment and meat for an exertion-efficient hop-glide back to their vessel. Instead, they would be together, yet alone, as Klaarongah painfully jogged and walked her way—burdened with her surgical wounds and sizeable load—while Krawwgh strained and struggled as he flew, carrying the heavy ram carcass and the other cannon, looped around his neck. They both endured considerable stress, as they struggled on their homeward journey. And they adhered to the proper security protocols by being armed and wearing their encounter helmets. No predators or assassins would be able to surprise them now, as they remained in constant contact, and technically vigilant.

By daybreak, they had covered over 25 miles, and they agreed to stop and rest, as soon as the heat began to rise. It was only early morning, and the temperature was already above 90 degrees, Fahrenheit. It would soar to above 120. They were both exhausted, and Klaarongah was in pain. They searched around for another thicket but found none—though Klaarongah did spot some pretty thick mats of tumbleweed in the distance. They headed over to the thickest one and began shaking the sparse fronds to detach any small dwellers, like scorpions, tarantulas, and lizards hiding in the shade. Then, Krawwgh quickly dug another pit to bury and cool their water, after they'd both took liberal gulps. They pulled the clumps over and around themselves and the ram carcass, which they both greedily chomped on a couple of times for some needed sustenance. Then, they fell asleep, dreaming about luxuriating under the life pod's cool shower spray, and then nesting together in their comfy perch pillows.

It was approaching sunset when they both rose up, well-rested and hungry. They still had three quarters of the carcass left, and they would, with time, consume every bit of it before reaching their destination. Then, after a lengthy rest, they would step up their hunting frequencies to restock their walk-in freezer, and now, after experiencing two unreasonable and violent encounters with humans, they would be added to their menu, with no misgivings or remorse. They would hunt them down with the same robotic alacrity as the drones. For now, however, they messily dined and slurped water, until they were ready to relieve themselves. Then, they would set out into the starry darkness on the second night of their journey, with over 70 miles to go. Klaarongah felt livelier, lighter, and experienced less post-surgical pain than the previous night. This was reflected in her pace, as she was able to maintain a spirited trot for hours. For his part, Krawwgh was feeling friskier as well, and with his load being lightened nearly 30 pounds from their earlier dinner, he was flying faster and higher than before. As he thought about all the bio-chemistry and nutrition that governed life, and especially their current situation, he realized how fortuitous it was that all the living things their race had encountered, throughout the local star system, were based on DNA, RNA, and multitudes of very similar proteins. This was part of the reason why they could readily eat any life-forms on Earth, without any molecular or nutritional alterations. The other part was probably because of their own evolutionary development as rugged, apex predators.

They repeated their travel pattern for the next two days, averaging thirty-plus miles per night, while resting and feeding during the sweltering days. While this 100-mile trek across arid, scorching plains, would have been a perilous journey for any creature, Klaarongah and Krawwgh were able to take it in stride, because of their extreme familiarity with harsh conditions back on their home planet Kaarp, where even moderate climates easily reached above 90 degrees and where bigger and more perilous deserts than even the desolate Sahara, belted its equator.

XIV. And Yet Another Encounter!

Just as the first orange and gold rays of dawn glowed over the horizon, Krawwgh knew he was within distance to see the mirror-like distortions of the electro-magnetically shielded and camouflaged life pod. If they were really lucky, at least one large prey creature would be dead, lying next to the invisible ship, after unknowingly bumping into it and receiving a fatal shock. Unfortunately, he saw no carcass, but he noticed something else, instead. There were footprints and continuous drag streaks in the sand leading away, from the life pod's periphery. Someone had apparently dragged some carcass off into the distance. As he followed the faint lines and footprints, he suddenly heard a commotion. In order to observe the tracks, he had been flying quite low, so he set down behind a nearby out crop of boulders. He saw a small band of people swathed mostly in tattered rags, along with a few camels. He noticed a couple of rifles among them, but no jeeps. They were huddled around a campfire where a small deer had been dressed, and was now roasting. As he was reaching for his infrared cannon, Klaarongah snuck beside him. They silently dance-chatted and decided to wait and observe this pathetic-looking group of humans. Klaarongah noticed something different about them. She signaled Krawwgh to do his usual, and then follow her lead.

Krawwgh waddled off far enough to avoid detection, and then flew off in a low, long, trajectory, while once again, mimicking a vulture by lazily riding another thermocline high up into the sky, as if circling for carrion on the desert floor below. They were less than happy, that the stragglers had helped themselves to their kill, but they understood the overwhelming temptation and needs. In particular, Klaarongah had picked up on something different about these people. They seemed less arrogant, confrontational, and militaristic than the others, and also appeared to treat their females as equals. These were encouraging signs.

Klaarongah engaged her helmet's semantics and syntax interpretive features, setting the amplifier on maximum, then rose from her position behind the rocks, towering over them all. "Stop! Don't shoot and stay still!" she dance-commanded. The crowd was too awe-struck and terrified to do anything else, and Klaarongah had her cannon at her side, just in case. A scrawny young man was slowly raising his gun when she saw him and yelled, "You, stop! Don't shoot, or I'll incinerate you!" in his native Oromo tongue. With all the group's attention focused on the giant bird-being, before them, no one had yet noticed Krawwgh, who was flying ever closer to the group, ready to swoop over and fry or stun the people, as per Klaarongah's orders.

They seemed to understand her and willingly complied. She then asked who among them the leader was. A frail elderly woman stepped forward and nervously explained that their tribal leader had recently died in a battle, but that the tribe honored her with the title of 'Priestess' in part, because of her wisdom and age. She then asked Klaarongah if she was the leader from her far-away land. Surprised by the elderly woman's gentleness and respect, Klaarongah answered. "No, Mama. I am a visitor sent here many years ago, from a world among the stars." Many in the crowd gasped. They could not comprehend what the giant bird had said. The clever tribal leader was skeptical. She asked. "Now, how is that possible? You are such a large, magnificent creature, and the stars are but tiny lights in our night sky."

Realizing for the first time just how primitive, uneducated, and isolated these poor wandering nomads were, Klaarongah answered. "Believe me, Mama, those tiny lights are bigger than anything you can imagine—your own sun being but one among the multitudes—and they only appear tiny because, they are so very far away!" Upon hearing this, many in the crowd cried out in terror and humbly prostrated themselves, by falling to the ground on their bellies and faces, with their arms outstretched in obedient servitude.

Frightened along with her tribe at hearing such a fantastic thing, the old woman was about to bend down on her arthritic knees, when she stopped and smiled. "I see that you are a magnificent bird-being, but with no wings to fly. How could you possibly travel any distance through this huge, dark sky?"

Klaarongah was impressed with how observant and wise the priestess was, and mildly amused by her understandable skepticism, but as she was about to explain, a huge shadow loomed over the crowd. Many began shrieking and wailing in terror, as Krawwgh slowly circled over the crowd and gently landed beside Klaarongah. Through Klaarongah's helmet, he had been eavesdropping on the conversation and had heard everything. He decided that the old woman's flight question was as good a time as any to make his appearance. The frightened, primitive, and animistic crowd was now moaning and chanting in obvious worship to their newly found warrior-bird-gods as even the clever and skeptical priestess had joined them. With all the people now down on their bellies, Klaarongah and Krawwgh engaged in a quick dance-chat, to discuss their fate. For now at least, they would reconsider coexistence instead of annihilation. They also decided it would be simpler to assure peace and order among the people and help them cope, by letting them continue to worship them as gods. Because, after all, in terms of power and knowledge, they were!

XV. Living like Gods

As the chants of the terrified worshippers slowly subsided, Klaarongah commanded in a motherly way. "Arise, my children, and look upon us." She then gently helped the old priestess back to her feet, and sat her on a large stone nearby. "As I stated earlier, we both come from another world very far away." She then bent her huge neck down to give Krawwgh another loyal and loving eye-kiss, and he enveloped her in his giant, winged embrace. "I am called Klaarongah, and he is Krawwgh. He is my life mate and protector! Together, we visit your world to make things better for you. We could easily destroy you all, but we would much rather live among you in peace and loving harmony, as we teach you many things about yourselves, your world, and your place with us, among the stars. We have chosen YOU to be the future of your world!" She thoughtfully gazed around the crowd. "You must trust us and not fail your children!" Because of their extreme poverty, lack of any communications technology, and remote, isolated location, none of them were aware of all the destruction and death that had befallen the rest of the world. Instead, their fears and resulting hardships were generally caused by the challenges of just scratching out a hard-scrabble life on the unforgiving and harsh desert-savannahs. As Krawwgh and Klaarongah learned more about the tribe and humanity in general, they would come to realize what a fortuitous thing it was that they had stumbled into these primitive people, who had not yet fallen victim to religiously inspired dogmatic inflexibility and xenophobia—with the usual assaults on reason and secular civility prevailing.

In order to display to the tribe their investment of hope and trust, Klaarongah thought of a ceremonial gesture to please and assure the crowd. Seeing a young mother quietly nursing her infant daughter, she pointed at her and asked, "You there, young mother, what is your name?"

The shy young woman replied. "I am called Nbegwe, O Great One!" Klaarongah gestured for her to approach with her infant, then slowly reached her mighty forelimbs out to cradle the hungry and crying child. Trembling with uncertainty and dread, the young woman handed over her infant daughter to the huge and terrifying bird god, without so much as a clue of what to expect. Klaarongah tenderly cradled the precious little being in her powerful three-fingered hands and gently raised it up to her massive, tilted, and still-helmeted head, to gaze lovingly upon its tiny helplessness, while marveling at its adorable and remarkable beauty. The young mother nearly fainted when Klaarongah gently lifted the baby skyward and proclaimed, "From this day forward, this child shall be known as Ndula—TRUST—as in the trust that we have in you, and the trust you will have in us, YOUR GODS!" After that, she handed the screaming, but completely unharmed infant back to her deeply honored and greatly relieved momma.

During this touching display of trust and diplomacy, Krawwgh had been watchful but silent, and absolutely pleased at how natural Klaarongah was, as a charismatic leader. He could feel the fear and tension subside within the tribe, as she instilled this new relationship with them. And he knew his own role in this was to support her as an enforcer and provide security from insurgency or rebellion. His loving mate Klaarongah certainly knew this because, as physically intimidating and formidable as she was, NOTHING would inspire as much terror in other beings as watching Krawwgh dive bomb and crush some big creature, or see him lift skyward, some villainous thing, and tear it to shreds with his monstrous talons. Surely, he was someone to be respected or feared by ALL. Now, everything would cease, as all eyes turned skyward, whenever the huge and ominous shadow of his unfurled majesty glided overhead.

It was nearly noon, and both of the newly appointed deities were in dire need of rest after their previous ordeals and 100-mile trek. Klaarongah dismissed the clan, telling them to return to this spot tomorrow morning. They obediently disbanded and traveled together, southward. Watching them disappear into the distance, they both turned and did their special signal dance, causing the life pod to uncloak and lower the walk-plank. Then, they scurried up and into the vessel's interior and made a beeline, for a shower before a quick raid on the freezer and bedding down together, in a hastily joined nest of perch-pillows. For the first time in the days, since they had set out for this first-ever mating with ostriches, they were truly safe, secure, and comfortable back inside the invisible life pod, with all its technology. Now, within this sturdy and computer-vigilant cocoon, they could remove their helmets and armor and slumber in complete safety.

During their deep sleep, they dreamed about all the people, animals, and things they had encountered during their recent adventure, and how fortunate they were in surviving and prevailing during the ambush. Never again would either of them leave the life pod without their encounter helmets, laser cannons, or armor. Nor would they ever again simultaneously engage in work tasks while off the vessel. Only that way could they function at maximum security. They had to remember that their fellow krrughs were still counting on them to steward the new world and spread their dying seed. Klaarongah and Krawwgh were pleased and relieved that this peaceful, primitive, spiritual—but not dogmatic—tribe was among the few thousand humans spared by the drones.

Eventually, their dreams turned to their breeding mission, and what their children would be like. It was no secret that they hoped for fully intelligent and functional little beings that would grow and develop into large, fertile adults, capable of managing their new world and fellow creatures. However, despite their best efforts to scientifically nudge all the biological factors to follow these inspired plans, life was still unpredictable, and outcomes could not be guaranteed with any certainty. Even on the lofty plateau of scientific and technological accomplishments reached by the mighty krrugh,

DNA was NOT some simple and linear blueprint, but rather, an extraordinarily complex recipe for life, and when coupled with all the other intricate and integral bio machinery necessary for cellular and embryonic development, random variations and unforeseen results were certain to influence outcomes. And so, they peacefully slept and continued to dream, all the while hoping that their synthetic eggs and sperms, containing their purposefully engineered chromatids, would produce hybrids that would be fertile, favorable, and fraternal towards all life.

They awoke the next morning well-rested but hungry. They had demolished their remaining stock in the walk-in freezer, and Krawwgh, in particular, would soon experience severe hunger pangs if they didn't hunt soon. They scurried about the ship, completing their daily equipment performance checks as well as seeing whether or not any further communications had arrived from mission control, during their four-day absence from the vessel. As expected, there were none, and since all shipboard equipment was nominal, and the environmental data indicated nothing but improvements across the board, they donned their helmets and gear and left the ship. It was just after sunrise when they went down the plank and re-cloaked the life pod in its invisibility camouflage. As they turned, they saw them in the distance, slowly approaching. It wasn't long before both Klaarongah and Krawwgh could easily see that they were the same group as yesterday—the animists. They both sighed in earnest hunger and disappointment, knowing that their hunt would have to wait.

Already wearing her helmet and therefore readily able to communicate, Klaarongah strolled out to meet the old priestess, as she struggled on ahead of her tribe. She smiled brightly upon greeting Klaarongah and was about to get down on her crippled knees when Klaarongah reached out to hug her and stop her from the painful and unnecessary gesture. Assuring that the priestess was now steady on her feet, Klaarongah gently let go and then danced-explained that she should refrain from such behaviors in the future, as both she and her mate already knew of the tribe's respectful loyalty. Just then, Krawwgh's shadow cast down upon the tribe as all eyes looked skyward to watch him glide overhead. He landed at the far side of the gathering, opposite Klaarongah and the priestess, and retracted his massive wings then waddled among the crowd which respectfully parted, as he made his way towards his mate. Again with a loving gesture of unity, he enfolded Klaarongah's lower half in his giant wings, while she lowered her long neck down to touch beaks, and then eyes in another gentle eye-kiss. All this affection and tenderness they showed each other and the elderly priestess did not go unnoticed by the tribe. Most were quite touched by the gestures while others were confused, as they tried to understand the behaviors being displayed by such powerful and dangerous beings.

Sensing a growing silence and questioning stares, Klaarongah reminded them all that they were a loving couple who always worked and lived together, and that they would rule together as loving parents and teachers over this special tribe. "As long as you remain civil and respectful towards one another, and continue to trust in us while obeying our commands, we promise to love and look after you, while not interfering much in your day-to-day lives. There is so much we must share with you, so that you can go forward in your world without repeating the same tragic mistakes of all the others." Many in the crowd were already weeping with joy, upon hearing their new god, Klaarongah, express so much love and good will. She went further still. “During the days of the last cycle of your moon that my mate and I have since inhabited your world, we have encountered other tribes of people before you, and we now know how much oppression, death, and despair they have inflicted upon you.” The crowd gasped in awe at how much their new gods understood and seemed to care about their strife and misery. “This will end soon, as Krawwgh and I will see to it, EVEN IF WE HAVE TO DESTROY ALL THE OTHER REMAINING TRIBES!” At that, the tribe erupted in cheers and cries of joy and praise for them both. Krawwgh was a bit concerned with the scope of the promise made. He knew how much harder this task would be now, without the giant drones, but he knew Klaarongah was just and right to do so.

Both of them were growing famished, and about to politely take their leave of the tribe to go hunting, when a couple of male tribal hunters, having just returned from a successful morning hunt with both a pig and a gazelle strung up on their carrying poles, stepped forward. One of them—an older, grizzled-looking fellow—came up to the elderly priestess and whispered in her ear. This was a truly peculiar and somewhat disturbing behavior for Klaarongah and Krawwgh to witness, because in their society back on planet Kaarp, secrecy was largely an unnecessary thing of the past. All krrugh were supportive, honest, and open about their thoughts and emotions. After the man finished, the priestess slowly rose and turned to them. She humbly asked if they would honor them by joining in their feast. Even though Krawwgh alone could have easily polished off both carcasses, they did not want to dishonor the tribe by refusing the gracious invitation, so they happily accepted.

They sat around the hastily erected campfire, watching with curious delight while trying desperately to hide their gnawing hunger, as they enjoyed, but silently suffered, the savory aromas of the roasting meats. Filling the idle moments while they waited, and all the while assuming they had flown together on Krawwgh's mighty wings, the priestess questioned Klarrongah about their fantastic trip among the stars, and what she thought of their new kingdom on Earth. She seemed dismayed and then saddened, when Klaarongah stood and dance-responded, that they both slept for a long time as they flew here, because the journey was so long, you couldn't pack enough food or supplies to stay awake the whole time. She did not mention the invisible star-ship, nor the fact that, anyone would be driven insane if they had to endure being so isolated for such a long time. Her mood immediately brightened however, after Klaarongah told her how beautiful Earth was, and how fortunate they both felt in being sent here. They were delighted when, a couple of curious toddlers waddled over towards them and gently touched their scaly talons and feathery bodies. Klaarongah was overjoyed, as a plump, naked little fellow approached, and then spun around and plunked down on his tiny butt right in front of her. He then leaned back against her feathery-softness. His father was horrified and profusely apologetic, that his son had made such an overtly disrespectful offense, but Klaarongah waved him off, showing that no transgression had occurred. She cuddled and cooed at the smiling, thumb-sucking toddler. Krawwgh too, was soon set upon by youngsters, who marveled at his massive wings and muscular body. Gently, he'd engulf and hide them in his wings, or tickle their faces, while letting them bounce about on his giant toes, as he arched and flexed his talons.

Finally, the feast was ready. A young woman sliced off the first and biggest portions from each meat and handed them to Klaarongah and Krawwgh. They smelled wonderful, but were too hot for either of them to swallow as whole chunks. The priestess noticed they weren't eating and asked if anything was the matter. Klaarongah explained that she and her mate didn't have teeth or jaws to chew with, and had to swallow their portions whole, which at the moment were a little too hot. But as soon as they cooled, certain enjoyment would commence! Then, Krawwgh rose up and politely dance-announced that the rest of the clan should go ahead and enjoy their feast. They were a little hesitant at first, but soon their hungers took over, and they began enjoying the festive meal. Klaarongah's and Krawwgh's meals soon cooled, and they grabbed and swallowed whole their portions, savoring the rich smells, tastes, and textures as the large pieces slid down their throats and into their gizzards. Most of the tribe ignored the ghastly display, while a few stared on helplessly. Klaarongah and Krawwgh were beyond caring how they appeared to the simple crowd. It was painfully clear that some of them just didn't understand much about birds.

As they were finishing up, the noon-day sun was fiercely beating down on them all, and Klaarongah and Krawwgh hugged the old priestess and nodded in appreciation to the earlier ear-whisperer for the splendid meal. Klaarongah handed over the snoozing toddler to his worried father, and they all departed in various directions away from the now-extinguished campfire. Waiting patiently for the rest of the tribe to disappear again, Klaarongah did the dance that uncloaked and deactivated the life pods security systems, then started up the ramp. Krawwgh emitted a gentle honk to get her attention and then explained that he was still hungry, and going out on a quick hunt for something big to share. Klaarongah snorted, and then replied, “Okay, my winged beast, but don’t stray too far!” as she tauntingly strolled up the ramp.

After a short while, circling within another big thermocline, Krawwgh noticed the stream in the distance where he had fetched water before and decided to stop and slake his thirst. As he approached the familiar landmark, he noticed the stream’s flow was way down from usual. He swallowed the sanitizer pill and then, after lapping up all he could of the stream’s quenching relief, he set off to investigate the situation. He flew in a northwesterly direction a couple of miles, tracing the stream’s general direction, and spotted the answer. Somebody had built a small, crude dam. He saw the tire-tread marks nearby, and his anger began to rise. He knew it had been placed there simply to make water scarcer, for the animists. It was also likely that whoever did this was in league with those ambushing assassins they’d met only a few days earlier.

XVI. Armageddon at Last

As he studied the simple structure, Krawwgh easily determined its weakest points and pulled a couple of the base mud bricks out from beneath the rubble pile above, and the backed-up water started coursing downstream again. Since he was still armed with his laser cannon and wearing his helmet and body armor, he was more than ready if anyone dared to challenge or snipe at him. He leaped back into the sky to seek out a tasty pig or deer for Klaarongah and him to enjoy. It was nearly an hour later when he spotted a cluster of warthogs rutting through the dry soils, in the midst of some patches of savannah grasses. Krawwgh focused on a big boar tusk-digging at some deep and stubborn tubers. Krawwgh took notice of his position and started his attack. He drew in a huge breath and tucked his head back onto his body, and began his dive. The boar never knew what hit him, as Krawwgh rammed, breast-first at over 100 miles per hour, into the clueless prey. The other pigs squealed in absolute terror and scattered in multiple directions, leaving the half-crushed boar there, dead.

Krawwgh took a minute to clear his head, then waddled over to his prey. The boar was barely a quarter as big as the mighty gucks back on Kaarp, but he was still a fine specimen, and would provide them both with a couple of tasty meals. Luckily, for Krawwgh, he wasn't quite as heavy as that trophy ram he'd hunted on that bluff, only a few days earlier, and he didn't have to fly so far this time either. Once again, He grasped a foreleg and a haunch in his massive talons, and after several powerful, dust-swirling downbeats of his wings, he was airborne, and headed back to the life pod.

After their tasty and fulfilling dinner, Krawwgh told Klaarongah about the damn and together they began to devise a final, decisive battle to destroy the marauders. This would have to involve their new tribe, so it would build more unity among all its members, and give them the confidence to face and conquer adversity, while surviving together as a group. Only then could they really begin to rule and govern themselves. Both of them could have disappeared into the electrical and mechanical labs for a few nights, and assembled a surplus of laser cannons or conventional guns for the tribe to easily destroy their enemies. But they knew, that the mismatch of comparatively advanced and convenient technology with psychologically primitive societies had helped prompt the ruin of mankind. Therefore, it was something to be avoided at all costs. Instead, they would support and aid their tribe by remaining the sole-possessors and judicious users of any advanced technology leaving them to fend for themselves with their usual arsenal of rock-slings, bows and arrows, clubs, and the few rifles they already possessed.

With the new beginning that Klaarongah and Krawwgh envisioned for the tribe and all that would be left of humanity, it would start with lessons on personal and social awareness and teaching of equality and acceptance, while undoing any harmful prejudices and superstitions that pervaded their current culture. Everyone was to be considered precious and necessary to society, and anyone they should happen to conquer should be offered a chance to join the tribe, but killed if they declined. That way, the natural Darwinian fear and distrust of strangers would no longer matter, as they would now populate a world where no one was born a stranger, physically removed, and socially isolated from others. And when Klaarongah and Krawwgh revealed the truth about their real selves, and how there were no gods to worship, or demons to fear, this new monoculture would be free of religious delusions and irrational superstitions that had plagued humanity for so long. They would finally be able to rationally explore and share the staggering truths about themselves, their world, and the universe, as one. While individualism would still be recognized and strongly encouraged within the tribe, it could NOT come at the expense of the welfare of the tribe, its ideals, or the environment. Likewise, social justice was eventually to be extended to ALL SPECIES, not just humans, so that animal suffering and species endangerment would never occur again because of human activity. First, however, they'd have to help them win this FINAL BATTLE.

Klaarongah and Krawwgh went to sleep that evening in a hopeful mood, knowing that these lofty ideals could eventually be met, and confident that the tribe would subdue their understandable fears and rise, with the furor, focus, and will to triumph. Early the next morning, they rose and did a quick daily check on the status of all the vessel's systems. Then, they met with the entire tribe, down by the outcrop of rocks where they had gathered for yesterday's feast. Since it was Krawwgh who saw and then destroyed the dam, it was only natural for him to speak first. Once again, the crowd marveled at his many agile and nuanced motions, as his helmet instantly converted them into the words of their Oromo language. Not wanting to risk any offense or hurt feelings, he lied a little while telling them that he had gone to the stream yesterday after the feast, to fetch water and run a couple of tests. Once there, he noticed that the stream's flow had been reduced to a trickle. Naturally, this alarmed him, because he realized that the tribe also relied on the stream. At this point, many in the crowd were nervously shuffling their feet and murmuring, as they anticipated what he would reveal next. As expected, he then told the tribe that as he flew upstream he eventually encountered a hastily made, mud-brick dam. Angered at such a thing being done to his people, he quickly tore it down to resume the precious flow downstream.

Many of the woman in the crowd began crying and screaming in terror, as horrible flashbacks of rape and daughter abductions assaulted their memories. Now, they cringed in mortal fear of renewed hostilities. Many a husband or brother hugged and tried to console their women, as they shared the painful memories of their emasculated helplessness, and many deaths, at the cruel hands of the heavily armed villains, who often enforced religious conversions at the end of a gun-barrel or sword. Suddenly, a man in the crowd yelled. "Don't you see what you've done, O Great One? Surely, they will now come after us with everything they have!" Upon hearing that, more tribe members began to wail in misery. Krawwgh and Klaarongah were stunned to see how frightened and upset the crowd was, and a little disheartened to see that they had already forgotten their promise to them.

As soon as they settled down a bit, Krawwgh began again. "I am sorry for causing your endured atrocities and great fears to come alive again, and yes, I suspect they will come down here to punish you for MY transgression quite soon. But what has been done cannot be undone. Remember our promise to you. We will be at your side to battle them, and YOU WILL BE VICTORIOUS!" Upon hearing those words, many in the crowd grew silent as they tried for the first time ever, to picture in their minds what victory would be like. The long, sad history of their small tribe of no more than 3000 destitute but honest and proud nomads, was one of being constantly bullied and threatened off their lands, or raped and killed for the simple 'crime' of being considered uncivilized, because of their ancient and different beliefs.

A low murmur started out from the crowd, growing louder and more confident as they began chanting, "Death to the marauders! We ride to victory on the wings of our bird-gods!" Krawwgh looked over to Klaarongah, knowing they would soon be ready.

The rest of that long, scorching hot day was spent preparing for war. Many took off to find branches for making bows, while others sought vines and hemp to make the bowstrings. Most of the hunters got together striking off razor-sharp shards from flint rocks and made them into hand knives, spear points, and arrow heads. No one in the camp bothered eating a dinner that night, as they were too busily engaged with war preparations, and wanted to be lean and mean with righteous hunger when they meted out their just revenge. Those few lucky hunters that had rifles tended to their upkeep and happily shared their small reserves of ammo, while the camels were pampered and rested for the battle ahead. By sundown, nearly all of their weapons were ready, and many tribe members—male and female alike—were practicing kicks, throws, punches, and knife-lunges for the hand-to-hand combat they were otherwise certain to engage in. That sleepless night, Klaarongah and Krawwgh discussed battlefield strategies and decided on a multi-pronged attack. They would make clever use of their firepower in waves of return strikes.

Sure enough, the next morning after sunrise, a long, thin, advancing line of thousands of villainous rebels and camels led by a single machine-gun-mounted jeep, which sputtered about on bottled gas, moved towards the tribe. As was explained the night before, the tribe would always take the moral high ground, and under the white flag of truce, offer a peaceful and diplomatic alternative to the battle that was, otherwise, certain to follow. As promised, both Klaarongah and Krawwgh stood on either side of the elderly and frail priestess as the three of them bravely walked together, under the big white sheet. This clearly indicated that they wanted a truce and the chance to peacefully discuss things with the leader of the advancing army. Klaarongah and Krawwgh were in battle dress, with their encounter helmets, body armor, and infrared laser cannons—all in full display. Because of their two previous encounters with barbarous tribal leaders, Klaarongah and Krawwgh were not going to naively trust this band of bandits and thugs for even a second, so she reached one of her long fingers into her shoulder holster housing the cannon, and preset the timer and flux array patterns for a focused lethal burst, followed by a continuous non-lethal broad sweep, that would definitely repulse attackers and heat up many dense, hard objects, including guns. Then, she estimated the likely length of their dialogue and set the timer. As they got closer, the gunner in the jeep trained the machine-gun barrel on Klaarongah, remembering her from the failed ambush. Of course, Klaarongah had recognized him from over a quarter mile away as the one lucky coward that got away.

Boldly and arrogantly, yet another black head-scarfed 'General' began. "So now you devils from hell take up with the heathens, eh?"

Klaarongah fired back. "If you will remember, 'sir,' WE came down from your 'heavens' and after having studied mankind for several decades, these are the only humans worthy of our presence!"

Not surprisingly, the supremely over-confident general huffed. "I will not sit here a moment longer and listen to infidels from wherever, trying to interfere with the will of Allah and all his holiness, to either convert or kill these Kafiri!"

As the machine-gunner glared at Klaarongah through his gun sight, aiming up on one of her big eyes, she snorted and then said through her helmeted features, "More likely, so that you can rob them and then run off with their little girls!"

Upon hearing that the general reached for his pistol to reply, while the machine-gunner began to press the trigger. In a blinding blur of beak, talons, and feathers, Krawwgh had leaped up over the jeep's windshield and knocked the gunner completely out of the vehicle and onto his ass. Then, after bending the machine-gun's barrel, rendering it useless, he dove down on the stunned gunner and fatally stabbed him with his massive beak. Meanwhile, Klaarongah had knocked the old priestess to the ground just as a hail of bullets erupted in their direction. At this point, Klaarongah's infrared laser cannon flared on, promptly singeing some of her flank feathers and instantly irradiating the general, his jeep, and many of his bandits arrayed behind him. The mighty general was completely burned in half, and many of the others were badly burned or recoiling in pain from the invisible heat waves that continuously pulsed and fanned out from the powerful laser. A few of the determined thugs reached for their guns and knives, only to find them far too hot to touch, let alone aim and fire. From around the large rocky formation in the distance, sprang two lines of tribe members, with rage in their hearts and murder in their eyes. They took off in opposite directions, sprinting towards their vile enemy. As the general's bandits split and turned to fire upon the engulfing forces, a huge volley of spears and arrows rained down on them, killing and wounding many, and causing some to flee, only to be mowed down by another volley. The tribe shouted, "Death to your god, and death to you!" They ran with wild abandon, encircling the terrified villains.

Hand-to-hand combat ensued. It seemed the tribe's empty bellies and long screaming chase onto the battlefield only invigorated them, as they overwhelmed and slaughtered most of their combatants. Krawwgh and Klaarongah assisted with the killings. Together, they punched, kicked, gouged, and stabbed the villains without any remorse or restraint. Less than an hour later, over 2000 corpses littered the blood-soaked sand. This number probably represented over a third of the humans now left alive on Earth. The tribe had lost 29 brave members, including two women and the priestess, Mama Mbanda, who likely succumbed to a massive stroke from all the intense commotion and her advanced age. There were no wounds or other noticeable injuries on her. As the crowd gathered around their brave and fallen leader, Klaarongah and Krawwgh joined them, and when it was their turn to honor the great chief, the two of them in unison removed their helmets, bent down in respectful closeness, and then together, one on each side, gave her a gentle eye-kiss of love and gratitude for all she had done for them and the tribe. Afterwards, they joined in mourning the remaining brave 28 and helped with burial details, though they both made mental note of the location of the mass grave for the buried enemy corpses. After these details to honor their fallen warriors were completed, Krawwgh corralled a group of younger tribe members and told them. "We can't rest just yet, my beloved tribe. Those who fled must be found and offered a chance to live peacefully among us, or be executed. Because if they should refuse us, they will only slowly fester and rot with nothing but hate, to accompany them in their tragic deaths."

Many of the young men looked confused and bothered by the compassion shown by their Living God for the welfare of the vicious cowards. "Forgive me for questioning your will, O Great One, but why should we care about the welfare of those so obviously unworthy and evil towards our tribe?"

Krawwgh unfurled a wing and patted the questioner's back, as he explained. "No one should ever be beyond a chance to right a wrong and do good again to others, while he or she is still alive. If they will not listen to reason, however, we cannot waste all our precious resources and time, trying to change their minds." Then, while he dismissed them all. "I know you will do your best!" With that said, the young men bowed respectfully to Krawwgh, and left. Sadly, almost a full day later, only a few of the villainous deserters would chose to join the tribe, as the rest couldn't let go of their religious indoctrinations, nor face the righteous scorn and loathing from those they previously shamed, in the past raids they had committed on this 'lowly' animist tribe. At least they were offered a chance.

XVII. Peace in the Valley—for Now!

Several days after the battle, and after the burials of fallen comrades and the big victory feast, the tribe was settling back into its usual routines of life—finding food, cooking, cleaning, and raising children. Not surprisingly, Klaarongah took a particular interest in the latter, and politely insisted that they all become educated—and their mothers as well. All the women were excited about the opportunity to be in the different surroundings school would offer, along with the chance to learn new things. Klaarongah explained, not only would it entertain them but help develop good skills for thinking critically, and be better able to support the tribe and manage their households. Since the wonderful Priestess Mama Mbanda had been their medicine woman, Klaarongah decided to take on that role, too, until such time that she could find a worthy student to train. It was set then, all children would be educated, while all adults would be strongly encouraged to participate.

Late one morning for the first time in their ancient history, the formal classroom teaching of both children and women commenced. All in all, it was a fun endeavor, as the children thrilled at sitting with their mothers, practicing reading, writing, and arithmetic, while Klaarongah patiently wrote the letters and symbols of their Oromo language. She was sensitive and helpful to any of the class stragglers, no matter how old, while also able to keep challenging the sharper students. She was a natural at teaching, and she clearly relished the task. After a couple of pretty intense hours they broke for lunch, and Klaarongah sat and gaily danced-chatted with the women about all sorts of things. Then, she answered many questions about her life and home world, Kaarp. Afterwards, sex education would begin!

As one of the tribal boys volunteered to supervise the younger children's recess play, Klaarongah gathered the mothers and adolescence around to begin the course. She began the lesson by explaining that women did NOT have to become pregnant unless THEY WANTED TO, and as the stunned and giggling audience listened, she taught them about contraceptives and alternative sex acts that didn't ever result in pregnancy. As she continued, she placed a small metallic cube on the table that they had gathered around, and gently squeezed it. A very graphic and slowly rotating holograph levitated above it, and as the startled and amazed students gazed on, Klaarongah began the necessary descriptions and explanations of the human female and male reproductive systems, and how vaginal intercourse often resulted in pregnancies, depending on the woman's menstrual cycle. Klaarongah was nearly as fascinated to see the holographs as the women, pondering just how inconvenient it must be for human females with three separate orifices to tend to, instead of just one, as in nearly all female birds, including herself. Her contemplative amusement over their differing anatomies soon ended. For the first time in days, she began to worry about her own middle-aged body and whether or not she was pregnant, as both Krawwgh and she desperately hoped. They ended the lesson with the holograph showing a live birth, as Klaarongah kept on explaining what many in the group had already personally experienced. Some, several times! Tomorrow, they would learn more about their bodies—and men's, with emphasis on changes at puberty, and the dangers of sexually transmitted diseases, while touching on topics like family size versus food consumption, and tribal population controls to minimize negative impacts on the local environment and fellow creatures.

For his part, Krawwgh was also busy teaching—though in his case, he was out before dawn with the hunters. Afterwards, he'd explain all sorts of things about the fellow creatures of the savannahs and deserts, and how interrelated and interdependent all living things were. He went on to explain local ecologies, environmental relationships, and meteorology. From germs to elephants, he covered it all, and in doing all this he made it clear that all these creatures, cycles, migrations, and weather patterns, were the results of natural, and not spiritual, phenomena. Some among them openly struggled to accept this, but Krawwgh knew this was to be expected. They would be struggling for at least a while, to shed their primitive ways of assigning a super being's intentions to explain things, as he patiently revealed the truths about this NON-SUPERNATURAL, BUT AMAZING WORLD! After all, they still thought Krawwgh and Klaarongah were some kind of animal gods, who flew through the heavens together on his wings, and would probably go on believing that until they revealed otherwise.

To assure that any teaching tools they brought off their invisible life pod didn't 'disappear,' both Klaarongah and Krawwgh never let the items get out of their sights and made sure that the vessel's cloaking and security systems were on 24/7. From time to time, and as lesson's warranted, they'd treat the clan to various devices, like microscopes, telescopes, simple chemistry and physics lab equipment, and the mysterious holograph cubes, without revealing their origins aboard a hidden vessel. So mesmerized were they all by the astounding technology and convinced of their bird-god's powers, that none of them ever questioned the origins of the equipment. This introduction of technology was always discussed and evaluated between Klaarongah and Krawwgh first, however, concerning how to use and explain a device, and what it was the tribe was expected to learn from its revelation and usage. As they explained these many things, they constantly emphasized how all the other people, that used to live in the world, misused their lofty accomplishments in science and technology, while neglecting the studies of themselves and the impacts of their societies. This resulted in many horrible wars, the starvation of billions, and the damaging of the environment. Thus, resulting in the cruel and unnecessary extinctions of many of their fellow creatures. Then the tribe was told that they were sent to destroy all of mankind, then save the Earth and its other inhabitants.

"Why were we allowed to live, O Great One?" Asked Nbegwe, the young mother who had trusted in her, as she handed over her baby to be ceremonially honored.

Klaarongah tenderly clasped her hand, as she explained. "Because you were too close by the ostriches!" Stunned by such a blunt answer, the crowd gasped as Klaarongah continued. You see, my beloved tribe, ALL HUMANS were to be exterminated, so that the wars and pollution would cease, then my mate and I would repair the damages done to your environment and save whatever species, we could. After that, Krawwgh and I were to save the traits of our own dying species, by mating with your wonderful ostriches. Nothing but jaw-dropping silence greeted Klaarongah's statement. She immediately sensed the shock and resentment amongst the crowd, and interrupted the hushed murmurs as she then said.

"As Krawwgh and I learned more about you and your suffering plight, along with the fact that your culture was the only one left NOT contaminated by a tyrannical, unreasonable, and self-justifying religion, we became very glad you had been spared by our colossal drones and decided that you were worthy of being the NEW SEED OF HUMANITY!"

Now, many within the huge crowd seemed pleased and relieved at Klaarongah's thoughtful explanation and renewal of loving intent, but others were still mulling over the shocking revelation while wondering what a 'drone' was. Someone in the crowd yelled. "What gave you the right to kill all the others?" The crowd let out another loud gasp, and became a sea of frightened murmurs and whispers. Heads everywhere swiveled around, trying to discover who had asked such a bold, authority-challenging question.

Klaarongah used the palm-down gesture to restore order and quiet, as she then answered. "I don't know if we had any 'right' to intervene in your world, but if we hadn't, you likely wouldn't be here now, as your tribe succumbed to either the repeated genocidal raids of your now-vanquished enemies or poisonous radioactive fallout from the other countries, in their nuclear wars. As my mate and I have told you often, you live on a rare and precious world, teaming with many diverse species, who have the same right to survive and thrive as you. All those who were exterminated were busy killing and starving one another, while carelessly causing the extinction of many of their fellow creatures. Above all else, our world decided that they could not let such an unnecessary and horrible thing happen, so…HERE WE ARE!"

Then, someone else yelled, "We weren't given a chance to change, before you killed us off!" At that, the crowd fell silent and many among them turned to face Klaarongah—expecting a furious response.

Instead, she bellowed, “When? After discovering you and your societies, our leaders waited decades, desperately hoping that humanity WOULD change. Meanwhile, our own extinction crisis was growing ever-closer.” Again the crowd grew silent, and the debate seemed settled. No one else challenged her, as many approached and held their children up to her for a loving eye-kiss goodnight, while giving a respectful nod to Krawwgh, who was now perched on a table nearby.

XVIII. Back to the Business of Babies!

It had been a month since the successful mating with the ostriches. So far, Klaarongah hadn’t noticed any changes in her body that might indicate a pregnancy. Of course, they both knew that the incredibly stressful events of the ambush and tribal battle could interfere with conception or lead to a spontaneous embryonic reabsorption, though Klaarongah had been vigilant to notice and report such things. As of yet, there had been no signs of anything going wrong. They both were very curious about the female ostriches that Krawwgh had inseminated, so he got on the life pod’s big screen and began tracking the tiny transmitters he’d harmlessly implanted in them, during the copulations. The signals were strongest at a point not far from the previous rendezvous and site of the ambush. They were pleased and decided that, early tomorrow morning, they would run out there and attempt some more intercourse, to increase the odds of a conception.

Before dawn the next morning, but after they had already performed their usual ship duties, Klaarongah inserted another set of artificial eggs, while Krawwgh festooned his penis with his engineered sperm syringes. They donned their encounter helmets and body armor, while carrying their laser cannons and Krawwgh's costume down the ramp and into the cold pre-dawn. Then, the life pod was secured and re-cloaked. Krawwgh looked over at his lover and silently danced, "Are you up for a little hop-glide this morning, sweetie?" To which she teasingly danced.

"Only if you think you can catch me, old man!" And with that, she sprinted into the darkness. Krawwgh snorted a laugh at her playful taunt, as he gave her a minute's head start, then leaped into the air to chase her down and link up for their hop-glide.

It turned out that their pre-dawn departure did not completely escape notice. Mntangua, the grizzled old hunter who had whispered into the priestess' ear, was up to relieve himself when he heard very rapid and light footfall in the distance. He grabbed a pair of binoculars he acquired as a war souvenir and quickly raised them to his sleepy eyes. Adjusting the glasses for night-vision, he had expected to see a group of green-lit warthogs, or some small bush deer sprinting in the distance, but instead he could just make out the large form of Klaarongah, sprinting ahead of Krawwgh, as he approached her from behind, with his huge wings unfurled, and muscular talons extended. Mntangua nearly swallowed his tongue, as he saw Krawwgh mount her and then, with a couple of sweeping wingbeats, lift her completely off the ground. Next, he saw Klaarongah reach out her mighty legs and powerfully spring-up, when she touched-off the sandy plain several yards ahead. Three huge leaps later, and they were gone out of sight, leaving only tiny dust-swirls behind. He was dumbstruck at the speed, power, and coordination he had just witnessed. No longer feeling the urge, he returned back to his warm bag, in stunned silence.

An hour later, and they were honing in on the signal, as the sun's brilliance was breeching the distant horizon. Off to one side was another convenient thicket, of tall savannah grasses, and they were soon hidden within. They would repeat their earlier routine, except that from now on, they would only attempt the pairings one at a time, as the other wore all the security equipment and kept watch. Although there were now no humans left to ever again attack them, they might encounter a sneaky lion, determined cheetah, or group of hungry hyenas. Klaarongah would go first, and after a couple of moments to mentally rehearse her female ostrich mimicry and 'psyche' herself up for the humiliation, she bolted out from the tall grasses and joined some of the other big hens pecking at grubs and beetles. Sure enough, that same big alpha male spotted her and began his wing flex display and chorus of throat booms. Once again, she played hard to get, as he grew ever more frustrated and aroused. He repeatedly pecked the ground and circled his sinewy neck. Finally, she was ready and promptly squatted, as he immediately sidled in behind her to do the deed. Klaarongah repeated the game for a couple of hours, until she was completely satisfied she'd received enough of his seed. Now, it was Krawwgh's turn, as she helped him into his ostrich costume.

Expecting the alpha male to be fatigued after his several couplings with Klaarongah, he went even easier on the spent but belligerent ostrich, as he sparred and lost, then sparred and lost again, before finally sneaking up behind one of the willing, subordinate females. He had to work quickly with each attempt, in order to avoid unnecessary battles with the alpha male. He would sneak up behind a female, uncap one of the syringes on his penis, then shove it in, and began thrusting all the while getting basal temperatures and testing each bird's cloaca for signs of conception from their previous mating. By the end of the day, they learned that none of the female ostriches was pregnant yet, while having mated successfully three more times. Spent, frustrated, but still quite hopeful, they returned to the relieving shade and seclusion of the tall grass and rested, knowing that at least for now, they had again given their best for the continuation of their species.

While resting and watching their simple but amazing mating partners, they both sat silently, wondering what their children would be like. They knew their highly selected eggs and sperms with their retinue of genetically engineered DNA-sequences couldn't guarantee which traits would dominate and present in the offspring. That would be determined by all the incredibly complicated series of events that randomly shuffled the gene locations on each chromatid formed during the sex cell's meiosis stage. Despite all their scientific and technological ability, there was no guarantee that the encephalization process would work, and present with the desired krrugh brain-development traits, in any of the hybrid chicks. Could this part of the mission be considered successful, if none of the hybrids developed the usual level of intellect and predation abilities, natural to all krrugh? What was to be done with them if they could not fend for themselves? These questions, and others, lingered in both of their minds, as they stared at the marvelous birds and hoped for the best possible outcomes. Whatever these final results were, they had to make certain that the hybrid creatures didn't pose any threats to the local ecologies, or somehow create an unnatural extinction of another species. They also knew that to ensure all this, they would be busy the rest of their lives with continued analysis, field observations, and corrective interventions.

In review, they had completed the most important mission objectives of ending all pollution, remediating all the resulting environmental damage mankind had caused, and the preservation of many endangered species. The only deviation from the mission objectives was, the preservation of a small nucleus of humans to inspire and educate on how to be responsible and thoughtful caretakers of their repaired world. In addition, if they could successfully breed hybrid creatures that could carry on the lofty ideals and accomplishments of their dead and dying culture as well that would beautifully conclude a highly successful mission.

XIX. Meanwhile, Rumblings and Grumblings Back at Camp

While Klaarongah and Krawwgh had been away for only a day, there was a plink of discord growing among the camp's otherwise harmonious activities. It started with that grizzled old hunter, Mntangua, relaying some of his observations and musings. "Without caring to notify, they come and go at a moment's notice." His annoyance, clearly displayed, while Nbegwe listened, but did not respond. Then, he questioned her in his old Oromo dialect. "Where do they go, and why is it a secret?" He asked, puzzled.

"I don't know." Nbegwe answered and then added. "Maybe they're hunting or doing those water check things," she guessed, hoping her answer would satisfy him. But instead, he continued.

“If they’re hunting, why wouldn’t they take some of the hunters along? Do we hamper them somehow? And just what is a drone?”

Nbegwe only shrugged and thought further before offering. “Maybe, they are mating with the ostriches and want some privacy, you know?” Disturbed by the sudden rush of mental pictures he was getting, Mntangua shuddered at the thought of his warrior bird-gods engaged in such an intimate act with such wild and stupid creatures. Then he complained. “Why does the tribe have to stop everything we used to do and spend so much time learning about things that won’t make us money, or help us get nice things?”

Nbegwe laughed. “Where could you spend any money, you old fool. There aren’t any towns or big cities left now, because we’re the only people left in the whole world. Don’t you remember?”

Then she scolded, “We were left alive, because we were the only ones they considered worthy, so WE MUST NOT FAIL THEM!” Annoyed, Mntangua waved her off, and stormed off to bother someone else, perhaps, a more sympathetic ear. Nbegwe returned to her chores and darling baby girl, Ndula. Why the old fool was so restless and unhappy, she couldn’t fathom. Since Klaarongah and Krawwgh’s arrival within their torturous, nomadic lives, they were now well-fed, happy, and secure with only peaceful and bountiful days ahead, no longer shadowed with the fear of raids from any merciless marauders. Then, there were all the incredible new things they were learning. Truly, Mntangua was just a meddling old fool, never pleased by anyone else’s efforts, no matter how grand.

After he left Nbegwe, Mntangua meandered out by a stream until he came across a group of hunters—his younger neighbors and friends. They smiled and greeted him warmly. They were busy re-stringing their hunting bows and fixing arrowheads, quivers, and flint knives. He flopped down on a warm flat rock, large enough, to stretch out his stiff spine and started his complaining again, to no one, in particular. Shocked by his sacrilegious questions and musings, two of the young hunters rolled their eyes at one another, while they let him rant on. Finally, one of them could bare it no longer. "Papa, what are you driveling on about? Our warrior bird-gods have guided us in battle to an everlasting victory over our nemesis, shared in their bountiful hunts, and taught us so much that we did not know, while asking little in return. What more could we possibly ask of them?"

Mntangua sat back up and snapped back. "They must want something more from us—something secret or dreadful, perhaps!" Then, he added, "It's only natural."

Hearing all this, the younger of the two hunters responded. "You're just being paranoid, Papa. They said all they wanted was to live among us in peace."

Mntangua wasn't buying it. "Where do they disappear to each night? How come they don't have some great house or mosque for us to seek them out and worship?" At that, the two young men could only shrug their shoulders and sigh, as Mntangua lay back down and stewed.

Very early the next morning, still in the pre-dawn darkness while the camp slumbered peacefully, Klaarongah and Krawwgh returned—exhausted and hungry—to the life pod's secret location a few miles north. Their silent return did not go completely unnoticed, however. Mntangua had decided to camp alone at the base of a spire of rocks, close by. He was in a restless state and sleeping lightly, when he was awakened by something he heard. About a tenth of a mile away, he saw

Klaarongah and Krawwgh dismount from their hop-glide coupling. He reached for his night-vision binoculars and what he saw next, made him gasp. Klaarongah did a little dance and a series of waves emanated from the ground, then a small, shiny mountain appeared. Next, a plank descended leading up to a cave, and the two bird-gods disappeared into its mouth. Then, the waves reappeared and everything disappeared. He fell back on his ass and struggled with what he had seen.

He was completely awake now. He kept his eyes peeled in the same direction. It didn't take long for another apparition to reappear. Once again, the strange, shimmering waves were followed by the shiny mountain which burst open its cave mouth and out waddled Mighty Krawwgh—alone, this time. He leaped into the black sky and took flight in a westward direction. Spellbound, Mntangua hid but scrambled through nearby brush, following Krawwgh with his binoculars, when he was surprised to see he had landed in the nearby battlefield, at the side of the enemy mass grave pit. He felt his throat tighten and sphincters loosen, as he saw something he shouldn't have. Krawwgh raked the dirt above the grave with his strong talons. In less than a minute, he had clawed away enough dirt to reach the putrid corpses. He then stepped down onto the pile and felt around with his ghastly talons and took hold of a corpse. Then, he pulled it up to the side of the pit. Mntangua had to choke back vomit, as he witnessed Krawwgh stab the corpse's belly with his monstrous beak and start slurping its black blood. Then, he struggled not to faint, as he 'felt' the corpse's bones crunch when Krawwgh stood upon its chest and pierce the ribcage with his talons. Still frozen, he nearly fell over again, as Krawwgh lifted the corpse skyward and returned to the shimmering mirage that again disappeared in the sand. Truly horror-struck, he couldn't believe what he'd seen in these few minutes—things that would strain the credulity of many of his tribe. But somehow, he'd have to convince them.

Meanwhile, after enjoying their pre-dawn snack and then a quick shower, Klaarongah and Krawwgh settled in for a well-earned sleep, oblivious of the trouble to come. They were too involved with the process of perpetuating their soon to be extinct race, to worry with the misperceptions of one old tribal member.

XX. Banishment from Utopia!

It was a few weeks later, early spring, and so far, Mntangua told no one of what he'd seen, because the tribe loved and worshipped Klaarongah and Krawwgh, still feeling they were gods who loved them all as their own children. He had to provide the tribal council with proof. Most of the tribe didn't feel it was their business to know where their gods went at night, but nearly all would be shocked and deeply offended to learn, of their dining on the dead! With a devious grin, Mntangua schemed that after he told the tribe about all the things he's witnessed, they'd have to believe him that their bird-gods were really soul-eating devils, instead. Maybe then, at least some of them would want to break away from all this imposed learning and unquestioning acceptance and, instead, FOLLOW HIM back to the carefree and unschooled ways, of old. In the meantime, he'd continue his clandestine vigil and patiently bide his time to make his case.

As it turned out, Mntangua wouldn't have long to wait as an annual feast to celebrate the spring season was coming soon, and something big was about to change Klaarongah's and Krawwgh's lives, forever. One early morning, before assuming their usual duties aboard the life pod, Klaarongah was up, excreting and showering to prepare for the day. As usual, Krawwgh was still busy devouring his breakfast. After leaving the shower, Klaarongah finished drying under the heat lamps, when she became curious about her weight. She pressed a button on the side of the excretion chamber and a plate slid in the floor, revealing a weigh-scale. First, waiting to make sure it correctly zeroed in, then she gently stood on it and weighed herself. She repeated the procedure twice more. She pushed a display button on the panel and a chart of all her recorded body weights since she was awakened from hyper sleep was projected before her, with averages and anomalies noted. A flashing yellow asterisk was blinking by her current reading. It was encouraging evidence. She had gained eleven pounds since her last weigh-in. Thrilled at what this could mean, yet cautious and wanting to be certain, she quickly inserted a small thermometer into her cloaca and noted with rising glee, that the temperature was elevated—another positive sign. Lastly, she inserted a hormone analyses probe. The result confirmed, SHE WAS PREGNANT!

Honking excitedly, she went back to Krawwgh where he was just finishing up in the galley, and gave him the wonderful news. He was elated as well and clasped Klaarongah's legs in his massive wings and lifted his much bigger mate right off the floor. They spun around, deliriously happy. At last, they would finally have a child to share all their love, joy, and wonder within this new world. Surely, this was yet another momentous occasion in their adventurous lives together, and a hopeful beginning for the final mission objective. Next, they scurried down to the bio-lab to find out how far along she was and to determine the sex of their hatchling. Whatever it was, they were going to be loving and proud parents of their interstellar, hybrid infant—the hope of a dying species! They finished their duties and then headed out to their beloved tribe to share the wonderful news.

Upon hearing the news many of the women and children in the classroom jumped, laughed, and cried. They tenderly hugged Klaarongah and then Krawwgh, who had decided to hang out with the class this morning. Soon, they all returned to their seats, and Krawwgh began his class about basic mathematic principles in every day usage. The rest of that special day seemed to glide by as both Klaarongah and Krawwgh dreamed about the new addition to their lives while teaching their bright and curious pupils.

With the entire campsite in a jovial mood, as they prepared for their annual Spring Feast, it was all too easy to end up distracted. After spending a long wonderful day and evening in the company of the jubilant tribe, the first-time parents-to-be said their goodnights and retired to bed. As always, they waited for their obedient and unchallenging crowd to disappear into the distance, before de-cloaking and then boarding the life pod. Klaarongah, for entirely understandable reasons, felt hungry and fatigued. She decided to bed down for the night, while Krawwgh went out and dug up something to eat. Since the tribe had left quite a while ago, and it was very late and dark out, Krawwgh felt that the vessel's secrecy would remain intact during the short excursion. He left the vessel without re-cloaking and headed off to the nearby enemy mass grave again.

In the distance, safe and undetected, Mntangua saw the 'mirage-mountain' open its entrance and disgorge Krawwgh. He flew off in the same direction as before. Mntangua watched his short flight through his night-vision binoculars again, only to see him land at the enemy mass-grave site. Then, he saw him start clawing and digging again. He knew only too well what Krawwgh was up to. As he sat there and schemed, he decided to risk discovery. He dashed toward the life pod's ramp, and then ducked into the entrance. Since Krawwgh hadn't reactivated the security systems, no alarms or security cameras were triggered by the intrusion. Mntangua knew he'd been incredibly lucky so far. He shivered from both fear and cold, knowing that he might be discovered any second. He was barefoot and dressed in only a flimsy shirt and pants, as he tip-toed to a nearby room and peaked in. Once inside, he became spellbound, as he saw so many strange things that he couldn't begin to understand. He stared at the star coordinate charts and colorful planetary maps and then recoiled in disgust, as he saw life-size posters of an ostrich and a human—both turned inside out. He tore down the human anatomy poster and folded it under his shirt—certain that it would implicate them in some morbid crime.

While his heart thumped, he crept down yet another curve-walled hallway. Directly ahead of him, the 'cave' branched in two directions, so he decided to turn right. That's when he saw her—the Mighty Klaarongah—asleep on a nest of big, colorful pillows suspended in a huge hammock. Then, he noticed something else. She wasn't wearing her helmet or armor, and as the seconds ticked by, he realized she was really nothing more than a big ostrich—a creature he'd hunted and eaten many times before in his long life. Smiling an evil grin, he fantasized about killing her with his powerful bow, and proudly strolling into camp the next morning with her head in a big sack. Then, Nbegwe and those arrogant youngsters would know who was boss!

Mntangua's murderous dream was suddenly shattered when Klaarongah gaped her monstrous beak in a big yawn and reached for a pillow with one of her formidable arms. He ran back towards the ramp to hastily exit this cave of other-world horrors, when he heard some commotion outside. He slid to a halt on the smooth, cold floor and huddled against the wall to avoid being seen by Krawwgh, who, fortunately for him, was engaged in dragging a corpse backward up the ramp and, thus, totally unaware of the intruder. Instinctively, Mntangua got down on his hands and knees and began crawling down the hall TOWARDS Krawwgh and the putrid corpse, while staying off to one side and out of his way. Then, he lay flat out on his belly and hid his face in the corner of the wall and floor as Krawwgh unknowingly pulled his nighttime snack over Mntangua's flattened physique. He nearly puked as the cold, putrid corpse slid over him in the dark and chilly hallway. He heard the hum of motors, as the ramp began to slowly close. He glanced back at Krawwgh, who had turned and was facing away again, preoccupied with log-rolling the corpse toward Klaarongah in the sleep chamber. Mntangua got back up on his hands and feet to crab-walk as fast as possible before rolling off a side of the rising ramp, and then falling a couple of feet to the ground. HE'D DONE IT! He sneaked on board and escaped without being discovered. He lay there completely still, and caught his breath, while he smiled about his close call escape. Somber reflection immediately returned, however, as he pondered all he'd seen and what he would tell the tribe soon at the Spring Feast.

Krawwgh was up early. As he was returning from the excretion chamber, he noticed the security system's status light was not glowing with its usual green 'on' indicator. HE HAD FORGOTTEN TO REARM THE SYSTEM last night, after retrieving their late night snack. Immediately, he armed the system with his pointed beak. Since the system had been disengaged, there was no holographic hall camera footage of an intruder. To check for theft and damage, he would have to wake Klaarongah and perform an entire intra-ship inventory and inspection. He gently woke her and filled her in. They both knew that if someone had gotten onboard, there was very little he could do to damage the ship, but theft was another matter. Depending on the item stolen, damage and death to the tribe could be severe. In any case, prudence and protocol demanded an exhaustive, thorough inspection. Since it was an early Friday morning, they were lucky the tribe wasn't waiting for them to teach classes or hunt and damn lucky the ship's invisibility device automatically re-cloaked the vessel, shortly after Krawwgh's return.

As they toiled away setting up and then scanning the entire vessel—starting with the most vulnerable and vital areas—they both felt ashamed at causing another breach of security. Once again, they strayed from their rigorously cautious training and were proving indeed, to be the 'weakest links' in the mission. Placing the undersides of their big beaks together, in a sign of their renewed unity for the mission's complete success, they would rededicate their efforts from this point forward.

After scanning every nook and cranny in engineering, they could correctly conclude that nothing was still onboard and that no damage had occurred to any of the vessel's propulsion and guidance equipment. It remained fully operational. As they moved onto the laboratories, they soon discovered the missing human anatomy chart. Hours passed, as they continued searching for other thefts, and were delighted, yet puzzled, when they confirmed nothing else was missing. This likely meant that whoever was on board last night, wasn't there for very long and possibly frightened away. But as they finished scanning the hallways with their broad spectrum scanner-wands, they detected very faint, latent-heat hand and footprints on the ramp, hallway, and surfaces right outside their sleeping chamber. Someone had been watching at least one of them UNARMED, VULNERABLE, AND ASLEEP! This could never be allowed to happen again. As they stared at the footprints outside the sleep chamber, they noticed they were pretty big and likely from an elderly male, because of an obvious hammertoe. Instead of subjecting the tribe to a traumatic investigation into the theft, they would quietly scrutinize all the males at the feast, paying particular attention to their feet. They spent the rest of the day together, but alone onboard the life pod, reviewing all their security protocol. Then, they reviewed all the messages they had received from their now-dead families and mission control to motivate and reinforce their commitment to the mission, as they polished off the tasty corpse. Tomorrow would start another school week for Klaarongah, while Krawwgh continued his hunting and field-teaching with the men.

Krawwgh was up very early the next morning, running his three in vivo ostrich cloaca samples again, in hopes that at least one of them might have given a false negative. After waiting a few anxious minutes, he had his results. None of them were pregnant, despite their repeated and exhaustive efforts. This made Klaarongah's pregnancy that much more crucial for the survival of their race, while necessitating extreme measures to protect the ovum. Of course, he knew his mate would provide their baby with the best of nurturing and prenatal care, but his three failures were unacceptable. That meant he would have to continue discovering and troubleshooting cellular and biochemical incompatibilities, while also greatly increasing the frequencies of mating, and number of partners. Since both

Klaarongah and he were so broadly immune to many diseases and had been comprehensively immunized for added protection, there was little risk of contracting and spreading any diseases, including STDs to their unborn, but the risk was not zero. From here on out, he would have to use precautions when even caressing his vitally precious and pregnant mate. He would have to step up his anti-parasite measures as well. His deepest fears were relegated to the future for their offspring. Would there be at least a few of them to love each other while sharing their new world? Would they differ enough from the ostriches or one another to mate and create viable, healthy offspring? Only continued efforts and time would tell.

Finally, it was The Spring Feast. The camp was in a festive mood as many among them sung and danced, often including their enthusiastic bird gods, while many tribe members sat in stunned silence, as Klaarongah and Krawwgh engaged in incredible feats of synchronistic agility while performing courtship rituals and 'happy dances.' When the bountiful feast was ready, the thoughtful preparers presented Klaarongah and Krawwgh each with a freshly killed uncooked pig for the main course, and a salad of various roots and grasses, followed by a small tray of pebbles and rock salt for their digestion. They were touched by all the delicious and thoughtful generosity showered upon them, and at one point, rose together to thank them all, personally. The huge crowd then grew quiet, as they joined their gods in relishing the feast.

Several hours later, the entire tribe had moved out from under their huge tarps where they had feasted earlier, and were now out at the original campsite with a roaring, crackling fire staving off the night air chill. It was there, by the flickering flames and reddish-orange glowing embers, that some of the tribal elders stood up one at a time, to tell scary tales or share hunting adventures—mostly for the entertainment of the very excited and spellbound children, as they sat at the feet of each storyteller. After a couple of scary tales and exaggerated adventures, most of the children went off to bed. Mntangua scanned the crowd, noticing that only a few teenagers remained among the big group. Nervously, he stood up and took his place in front of the slowly dwindling fire, to face Klaarongah and Krawwgh. It was just then that they glanced at his large bare feet and noticed the prominent hammertoe. He stuttered, trembling in terror, as he began his accusation. "M-my t-tribe, you have been deceived by these t-two b-beings! D-do not be so gracious." He then raised a shaky arm and pointed at Klaarongah and Krawwgh. The whole crowd let out a gasp and then a calamitous din of indignation and outrage arose.

Absolutely incensed, Nbegwe shouted, "Mntangua, you old FOOL, what has gotten into you now?"

Growing in his own indignant confidence, he responded. "Only this, my dear sister. We look up to these two…beings with so much respect and worship, yet we know practically nothing about them—or at least YOU don't know much."

Then, one of the outraged young hunters yelled, "Shut up and sit down, you stupid old man, and keep your evil to yourself!" For their part, Klaarongah and Krawwgh remained calm at the infuriatingly disrespectful tone and only stared back at their bedraggled and pathetic accuser. But the crowd of younger men—his fellow hunters and friends—crowded around him. Raising a mighty wing, Krawwgh stilled their threatening advance and dance-spoke through his helmet. "Wait! Let us all hear what this man has to say." The men immediately obeyed and left Mntangua alone. Krawwgh looked at him. “You were saying?” Surprised by their willing patience to hear his charges, he continued his accusations.

“Y-you c-come and go often and with no announcements or warning, and then you—OUR SUPPOSED GODS—shamefully mate with those lowly ostriches. The same stupid creatures that bury their heads in the sand and that we are now prevented from hunting.”

Indifferent to his tone, but annoyed at his ignorance, Klaarongah corrected him. “Ostriches don’t bury their heads in sand, Mntangua. They lay their necks down on it to warm themselves.”

Deciding that, now was the time to present his stolen evidence, Mntangua reached into his shirt and pulled out the graphic, human anatomy chart and handed it to Nbegwe. “Why would someone have such a butcher’s chart, unless they use it to eat us?” Many of the women gazed on the chart and realized it was just another pictograph—a representation of the human body’s internal organs—for learning purposes only.

Then, someone in the crowd shouted, “We’ve used that chart to learn about our bodies, Mntangua.”

Krawwgh chimed in. “What other misconceptions trouble you, sir?” At that, the crowd started giggling and easing down its tensions, to the annoyance of Mntangua, who, then again pointed his spindly finger at Krawwgh and blurted out. “You dig up the dead and eat them—twice—I saw you, and you hide each night, inside a shiny, mountain cave you erect from the sandy ground. I know because, I’ve been in it.” The crowd stared at Krawwgh, in stunned silence, trying to process all these accusations, as Mntangua continued. “What kind of gods hide their temple from their worshipers, eat their dead, and mate with lowly creatures?” The crowd gasped in horror, with their rage building toward Mntangua, for hurtling such awful accusations at their loving god. Those same men circled Mntangua and started punching and kicking him. Krawwgh stretched out his wings and emitted a long, deep, and resonant honk, causing everyone to stop in their tracks. All eyes were on him again, with most of the men standing ready, willing, and eager to tear Mntangua to shreds, while hoping that Krawwgh's righteous rage would be confined on Mntangua only, because after witnessing many big-prey hunts with him, they knew what he was capable of.

Sensing her mate's growing anger and knowing better than anyone, just how powerful his wrath really was, Klaarongah took the opportunity to intervene and try to alleviate tensions, while explaining and reassuring their beloved tribe. "We often leave early in the morning and complete our traveling before the noonday heat, as we gather water samples from any streams or aquifers we encounter. And yes, my powerful mate and I are able to link-up and dash across your arid planes at considerable speeds, in pursuit of prey, or ostriches to mate." She slowly looked around the crowd and then continued. "When I joyously shared the news of my pregnancy, it wasn't by my mate Krawwgh, but by one of those 'lowly' ostriches." A hushed gasp emanated from the crowd, as many among them struggled to understand why they would ever really consider birthing and raising 'spawn' from such comparatively feral and stupid creatures. She was among them now, explaining, "As we told you earlier, we are the last of our race sent from our world, to yours, and all that is left of our mission now is to mate with some of your ostriches to preserve some of our species past glory! Whether or not you approve of them, ostriches are our only hope." Then, she got up in Mntangua's frightened face and leaned menacingly forward, as she asked, "After all we have done for the tribe, who are YOU to question our motives or methods?" Just then, some woman in the tribe cautiously approached, trembling and crying as she then humbly informed.

"But, Great One, if you eat the dead, their souls can't live and play in the spirit-world!

At that point, Krawwgh jumped back into the conversation. "Even though I am not so large as my beloved mate, my body requires much more food. Since the grave I picked to feed from, was your long-suffered, mortal enemies, we didn't think you'd mind. As we now see how this distresses you, we will no longer dine on ANY HUMAN FLESH! He exchanged a supportive and knowing glance at Klaarongah, then panned around the obviously stressed crowd. He added, "Unlike you humans, we evolved on a desolate planet as top of the food chain, carnivores. Between the anatomical limits imposed by our species gene pool, and our large nutritional requirements, predation was a necessity. On our harsh world, both prey and carrion could not afford to be overlooked as sources of food. Early on, our species learned of our fragile relationship with our fellow creatures and our obligation to protect them all—and the environment of our planet. We will keep teaching you these same life lessons and more." The tension in the crowd eased, then they performed the 'deactivation dance' and the life pod de-cloaked in the distance. It appeared before the stunned crowd like a crystalized mirage, and further verified some of Mntangua's accusations.

Meanwhile, Nbegwe gathered her tribal elders together, in a quick meeting, aside from the crowd, to decide Mntangua's fate. Not only had he insulted their 'living gods' by directly accusing them before the entire tribe, he also trespassed into their home, violated their tribal rights of privacy, and stole from them. Like everyone else in the tribe, he benefited from the battle victory that Krawwgh and Klaarongah helped them secure, and had dined freely among them all, on the bountiful hunts they willingly shared. While some of his accusations ended up being true, their mean-spirited and conspiratorial nature meant that he didn't trust these beneficent beings, despite all they had done for the tribe, and so, Mntangua could no longer be considered a trusted member.

Finally, Nbegwe arose from her squat with the other tribal elders, and faced the rest of the tribe to issue the verdict. "The council of elders and I have decided that Mntangua can no longer be trusted by the tribe, so he is now cast out from us!" Upon hearing this, Klaarongah and Krawwgh remained stone-silent, feeling that the punishment was a little harsh. But it was fair, and they knew how important it was for the tribe to practice governing themselves and respect the judgments given by their elected officials. As for Mntangua, he knew what this meant. Tomorrow at dawn, he would be given a water bag, some food, and a pair of sandals for his journey, forever away from the tribe that once loved and honored him. At first he cried out, begging for mercy, but as it became clear his pleas were falling on deaf ears, he got angry and then defiant. As they dragged Mntangua away from the smoldering campfire, he yelled and screamed that the two bird-gods were really devils sent from hell, and that they all would burn for eternity. His words revealed just how contaminated his poor mind still was, by religiously inspired superstition.

XXI. Making Way for Baby

Life for the tribe quickly returned to normal after Mntangua's banishment and most mornings after their usual life pod duties, Klaarongah gathered a class of eager children and their mothers together to learn, while Krawwgh would leave earlier in the morning to go and hunt with the hunters. In the evenings, Klaarongah and Krawwgh would regroup onboard the now-revealed life pod with Nbegwe and various tribe members to join them. Whenever possible, Krawwgh adjourned to the bio-lab and continued his fertility research, desperately trying to find out why his engineered sperm weren't fusing with the ostrich egg cells.

Being her first pregnancy, Klaarongah was ecstatic to be in this condition, but also aware of her middle-age status. While in many ways she was still in her early prime for a life-span that averaged 120 years, she was quite old to be having her first pregnancy however, and all because of the decades it took for them both to reach Earth. Although she was one supremely tough and powerful being, she knew she needed to protect this special pregnancy as best she could, by taking things easy and allow Krawwgh to do all the hunting. She gorged and rested frequently, reducing any risks or stresses on their unborn. Either Krawwgh or the hunters would bring her a fresh kill every day, and Krawwgh always offered her the liver or other choice parts of his dinner as well. As expected with any healthy pregnancy, Klaarongah continued gaining weight and became quite plump.

In addition to her prenatal responsibilities, she and Krawwgh would often group the tribal elders around the big flat rock where beloved Priestess Mama Mbanda used to sit, and teach them governance ideals while discussing tribal problems or news. Topics often involved lessons learned from the mistakes of all the other previous people in the world and how they misapplied too much of their technology for convenience and warfare, while not spending near enough effort to learn about themselves and one another, in order to peacefully and productively coexist. Anyone was allowed to join in these discussions, and what would start as usually just the elders often swelled to most of the tribe not already bedded down for the night. Klaarongah and Krawwgh explained that gross over-consumption and overpopulation contributed to many of the problems in all the past societies on Earth, and that those situations should never be repeated. These new humans were to become smarter, more contemplative, and analytical whenever they approached and solved their tribal needs. Given enough time, they would proudly discover many technical things as they applied their newly learned critical thinking skills to answer nature's questions, while using well-reasoned lessons in ethics, psychology, and sociology to establish and enforce a good, all-inclusive society. Some of the main things Klaarongah and Krawwgh passed on, were the vital ideas of remaining a small population of nomadic hunters who knew enough not to overhunt or fish any area, and not spoil or pollute its local ecology by settling down, domesticating animals, and cultivating large crops. Then with time, if the population got big enough to form splits or branches, every effort had to be made to remain in touch and familiar with one another's cultural and language changes, so they wouldn't become estranged! This way, they could avoid instinctual suspicions that might lead to conflict or war. Above all else, tolerance, compromise, and diplomacy were always preferable to aggression when settling any of the many inevitable disputes.

Finally, a little more than ten months since Klaarongah first learned she was expecting, she laid her egg. Other than a sense of building pressure, it was a painless procedure. But because she was of a very advanced age for her first pregnancy, the lining of her oviduct was less pliable than a younger female's, and the strain of laying her egg, caused it to tear loose from its ligaments and be shed along with the egg, leaving her permanently sterile! All this took place while Krawwgh was out among the ostriches trying yet again to impregnate any females he could. When he returned from his 'proliferation duties,' he waddled into the life pod, and blasted a short honk which she responded to with a soft caw. They gently eye-kissed and engulfed each other in a wing-and-forelimb embrace. Klaarongah rose up briefly to let her mate gaze lovingly on the big, beautiful, bluish-white egg.

So that he did not disturb the nesting pillows, he gently bent his massive head down to marvel at his shell-encased child. With great care, he tapped and sniffed the egg while admiring and committing to memory the smooth texture and scents. He wasn't the biological father, of course, but that didn't matter to either of them, as this little being was the result of their incredible efforts, committed love, and the hope of a dying species. Krawwgh was probably sadder than Klaarongah upon learning of her permanent sterility, if only because he knew what a loving mother and excellent role model she'd be for any number of chicks she'd be lucky enough to lay. At least she had one now and had experienced the wonders of pregnancy. Soon, there would be a brand new little being in their lives. Because they had so much medical testing and imaging equipment onboard, they already knew quite a bit about their baby and could assume it was healthy. But as the pregnancy progressed so too, did the thick and obscuring eggshell, and since they did not want to risk causing the ovum any harm during its development, they hadn't exposed it to any X-rays or other intrusive radiations just for the sake of learning more. All would be revealed when it was born. They could also have constructed a sophisticated and very convenient incubator, complete with thermo-regulators and automatic egg-turning devices as well, but instead, they chose to take turns, attentively nesting their egg, all the while furthering their bond with their future child.

Early one morning, they heard a ticking from inside the egg and delighted in knowing their baby was struggling to be born. Snuggled side-by-side in thrilled anticipation, they issued gentle caws and honks to encourage their little one. Soon, a tiny beak, much like Klaarongah's, had broken through the thick shell, followed by more of its little face, which began a vigorous chorus of peeps. Then, a talon poked through, followed by the rest of its downy-soft and furry little head. LITTLE HEAD? As the chick freed the rest of itself from the shell, two things became apparent. One, their darling chick was definitely female, and two, except for her big dagger-ended beak, her head was more ostrich-like, not krrugh. That meant the encephalization gene therapy had failed. Now, all that remained was to see how much, if any, smarter she was than an ordinary ostrich. Clearly, she would never become krrugh-smart. Nonetheless, they adored her and marveled at everything she was and did as they took turns nuzzling, eye-kissing, and enfolding her, while Krawwgh regurgitated some food for his brand new baby girl. As newborn ostrich chicks go, she was already quite big and agile, as she stood up and began flexing and stretching her oversized talons and forelimbs then clacking her comparatively big beak. Then, she craned her long neck to curiously gaze up at these two huge beings. They took turns gently snort blasting their daughter with warm, nasally exhaled air to her joyous and sensuous surprise while lying around her in the pillowed nest they'd made. They delighted in watching her climb over and scurry about the contours created by the arranged pillows and their supine bodies, until she tired and found a feathery-soft and warm little nest to cuddle into between them. This way, the three of them rested for a couple of hours, with Mama and Poppa lying very still to avoid crushing their snoozing darling.

The peaceful slumber ended when their daughter awoke and promptly announced her hunger with another chorus of tiny peeps. This time, Klaarongah did the honors. She gently opened and lowered her giant beak over her tiny daughter to reward her hunger cries. Despite her small brain, she was strong, active, and hungry, which pleased them greatly. She was theirs, and they loved her unconditionally. As long as either of them was alive, she would be safe, well-fed, looked after, and always doted on. Because they couldn't be sure that she would ever be able to learn and interpret their astoundingly complex dance-language, they decided to give her an oral name—Klengah—which means 'most curious one' in the language of the krrugh, and one of the few sounds either of them could vocally articulate clearly.

After two weeks cooped up inside the life pod, with only Krawwgh occasionally leaving to update Nbegwe and the tribal elders, or doing a quick hunt to feed his brood, they took their infant daughter out to meet the tribe. Immediately, Nbegwe, her sister Mnonga, and the rest of the tribe fawned over little Klengah as they eagerly awaited their turn to cuddle and pet the adorable baby bird. Already weighing 20 pounds, she was quite the bundle and could prove hard to handle whenever she started to fidget and squirm. The crowd marveled at how soft, responsive, and social she was as she went from person to person, expecting to be showered with loving attention. With each gentle stroke she received while sitting on someone's lap, her huge dark eyes would close in ecstasy, and she would rub her down-soft head under the person's chin and drift into a sleepy calm.

On and on this went until she spotted a gathering of children. Immediately, she fidgeted and squawked, demanding to be put down so that she could investigate these little beings. As soon as she waddled near the kids, they began smothering her with hugs, pets, and kisses. Once again, she poked her little head up on their chests and under their chins to rub up against them or gently pecked at their lips, expecting something to eat. They all adored her immediately, as they played with her under her parent's pleased and watchful gaze. Klengah's unbridled affection and curiosity enlivened the whole camp!

XXII. A World to Explore

It was late spring now, and on the southern Ethiopian Plane, things were starting to get unbearably hot for the tribe. Soon they would pack up their tents and belongings and head eastward through Somalia to the ocean and set up a new, seasonal camp there. All the tribe was in a festive mood as they anticipated, cool, lapping waves to swim in, warm sandy beaches to relax and play on, and the gentle relieving breezes of the shoreline. The hunters were retrieving the big fishing nets and sharp stone spears while the children were still enjoying school underneath the big tarps where Nbegwe and her sister taught important parenting skills. Klaarongah continued to amaze and delight them with some of the incredible facts and discoveries about the Earth, their fellow creatures, evolution, and their solar system. Many also studied Klaarongah as well, trying to understand how her helmet was able to 'read her dances and talk to them.'

Throughout those long days spent learning and preparing for their summer beach camp, little Klengah was brought along with Klaarongah and was free to explore the camp, though always under her watchful gaze. The infant would wander into the midst of the early morning hunters and then over to the busy mothers, attending to their own toddler-babies. Some of them would take time out to gently rub her soft feathers, scratch and rub her head and neck, or give her a big hug. The real treat for little Klengah was when she wandered into class. The teachers and even Klaarongah knew it was next to impossible to compete for the children's attention. Klengah was always as thrilled to see them as they were to see her, and she basked in their gentle adoration as the throng of little hands reached out to her, often with some piece of dried fruit or dates to chomp up and swallow. Some of the bigger kids would lift her up in their laps, and then let her poke her little head with it's pretty big beak up under their shirts where she would rest for a few minutes against someone's warm and smooth-skinned chest. Before long, she'd grow restless and wander off to someone or somewhere else, always under the watchful gaze of her big mama.

The 'darling of the camp' also had the attention of somebody else. Mntangua, the grizzled old troublemaker and recent outcast from the tribe, was lurking in the distance behind one of the large sandstone formations near the camp. He had been hiding in the camp shadows all along, picking through garbage to supplement his meager catches and kills. Day by day, he was growing more delusional. His twisted reasoning led him to hate Klaarongah and Krawwgh ever more for causing his ruin when he chose to confront them, that fateful day. Not long ago, he had been a respected and proud tribal member, a skilled and successful hunter, loved and trusted among all his fellow hunters and tribal women. Now, he was a walking dead ghost, no longer recognized by any of his former friends or family. Meanwhile, those two 'devil hawks' continued to be adored and worshipped by the whole tribe, while their little spawn co-mingled and caroused through the camp, joyous and carefree. The injustices heaped upon him were intolerable and required a planned and measured response. For now, he would bide his time and continue to shadow the tribe all the way to the Somali beaches and patiently await his chance to spring his revenge. He spent the rest of the day stalking the 'little ostrich' Klengah, dreaming about how much tastier her meaty thighs were going to be when they were seasoned with his sweet revenge!

After little Klengah had finished her morning rounds, Klaarongah walked her out to the flats just outside the south end of the camp, where they ran and played for hours. During all the spontaneous fun, Klaarongah was pleased to see how strong and agile her toddler was, and how normal her physical development seemed to be. Then, she decided to test her mental abilities by attempting to teach her some very simple 'dance-phrase' moves—the basics of their language. Specifically, she wanted to see if Klengah could learn enough simple phrases to communicate her needs. But as she deliberately gyrated and gesticulated simple words and phrases, all the while desperately hoping her daughter would begin trying to mimic her moves, all little Klengah did was blankly stare at her big mama in total incomprehension then run over to Klaarongah's legs and sit on one of her huge talons, signaling that she wanted another 'leg ride.' Clearly, her daughter exhibited no instinctive proclivities to ever learn their language! Truly dismayed to see this, Klaarongah was immediately distracted when she gazed down at her daughter who was looking up at her, eagerly awaiting her ride. Klaarongah bent her long neck down and gave her baby a loving eye-kiss, and then gently scratched her little head with her beak-dagger. Then, they took off together, with Klengah riding on her mama's talon as she ran back into camp.

Later that evening she told Krawwgh about Klengah. They were both saddened and worried about their daughter's future. While it was obvious that her social awareness and related skills were far beyond those of an ostrich, she would never be able to understand or communicate effectively with the tribe or any of her hoped-for siblings. This put even more pressure on them to continue breeding with the ostriches to give her some siblings for companionship and help. If they were ultimately unsuccessful, she would have to remain with the tribe for the rest of her long life, or spend it linked up with some group of ostriches that couldn't possibly be as stimulating and engaging as the people she was deeply bonding with. These were worrisome thoughts. Since they were both already middle-aged, Klengah might have to live many decades alone without their loving care or the company of compassionate siblings like herself. While these were real concerns, they were for another day. In the meantime, she'd always have her mama, daddy, and tribe around.

The camp was finally ready. They had packed up their tents and loaded up their five big dromedary camels—spoils of their previous massacre—and left. It would be a sixty-mile trek through southern Somalia to reach the shores of the Arabian Sea. Just as the tribe had been busy striking camp for the last few days, Klaarongah and Krawwgh had been busy with their life pod duties. After securing their precious engineered sperm and egg experimental samples in the bio-lab's cold storage, they programmed the vessel to use a low-power consumption plan. Its nuclear fusion reactor could operate smoothly and indefinitely without their involvement, constantly supplying whatever wattage was needed, while the onboard computer and security system would continuously monitor all areas, materials, and systems. To assure that no one could ever board the life pod in their absence, Klaarongah and Krawwgh rearmed the fatal shocking and invisibility cloaking devices, before leaving on their trip. The outcast Mntangua would surely die if he tried to sneak back onboard. Since nearly all the humanity left alive on Earth was contained within this happy, unified tribe, there was virtually no risk to the life pod but wanting to keep up with all their training protocols, they armed it anyway.

In order to provide a lookout for the tribe, Krawwgh would fly out ahead for a couple of miles then circle back. That way, he could update Klaarongah on anything occurring up ahead. Then, she would circle back to relay and chat with Nbegwe and the tribe. Since there were so many of them, and they all varied greatly in age, walking speed, and ability, stops were frequent. They had brought along much food and water and were well-seasoned desert travelers, so there was no urgency—just joyful anticipation.

One especially hot day, Krawwgh decided to treat his daughter to a ride in the sky. Despite her vigorously squawking protests, he gently but firmly clasped her in his talons and then took off into the sky with a few of his powerful wing beats. His 70-pound darling continued squirming and squawking in mortal fear, but as her big papa kept cooing to her with loving reassurance, gentle eye-kisses, and beak-play, she began to relax. He'd gently glide up the currents of rising hot air from the scorching earth below into the much cooler cross-breezes of the higher skies, then slowly circle back down toward

Klaarongah and the tribe. It soon became apparent that Klengah was enjoying the flight with all its sensations and the much cooler breezes. With her small forelimbs and legs poking out from between Krawwgh's beefy talons, she began flapping her little forelimbs and kicking the sky to help her papa. Krawwgh was deeply touched upon seeing this, so he circled back and swooped down lower, to show Klaarongah and the tribe. A little later on, Krawwgh regurgitated in his beak to provide Klengah with her first ever, inflight meal. They kept at this for a couple more hours until almost sunset which was when the tribe was going to strike camp for the night.

As Krawwgh approached for landing, Klengah instinctively put her legs out and bent her knees to help cushion the landing's impact, almost in a manner Klaarongah would use when she and Krawwgh went hop-gliding together. No matter how limited her intellect was compared to theirs, she definitely exhibited at least one krrugh-like trait. Tribe members quickly unpacked their bedding and dinner gear, while others rested the camels and began building a fire. Soon, most of the camp was resting their tired feet and waiting on a deer to roast while Klaarongah, Krawwgh, and Klengah dined on some freeze-dried warthog and salt cakes. The glowing warmth of the campfire felt wonderful against the chill of the cold desert night. After the camp finished dining, most began gazing skyward, marveling at the sparkling jewels of the Milky Way. "Show us your home world, Mama Klaarongah." She was touched by the child's inquisitive request, and put her helmet back on to give her an answer.

She stood up and answered. "My darling, you could never see our world from here, and for two reasons. One, stars are so big and bright that you can only tell if any worlds are nearby when they cause them to 'wiggle' and dim a tiny amount. And two, our solar system can only be viewed from the sky, facing the bottom half of Earth." Upon hearing Klaarongah's explanation, the young lady sighed and sat back down. Immediately sensing her disappointment, Klaarongah asked her to go over to one of the camp sacks and take out a long tubular package and bring it to her. The girl smiled and ran over to the big sacks of gear and searched until she found it, then happily skipped her way back to the seated crowd. Klaarongah patted her head and danced 'good girl,' then quickly assembled the small telescope. Because it was made by krrugh optical physicist specifically for the mission and utilized some of their quantum-indeterminate reflection and oscillating-polarization discoveries, along with the inverted star and planet light interferometer, they would be able to see any stars and their planetary systems out to a distance of about 2000 light years.

Since Klaarongah was very well-informed about their local star groups and the planetary systems that surrounded them, she delighted in patiently showing them the various systems, while sharing all sorts of fantastic and awe-inspiring facts about the ones they viewed.

Over an hour passed as she bedazzled the crowd about just how huge stars really were, including the very nearby sun. She explained how far away they really were by making the simple analogy of how tiny a man looks and how dim his lighted torch appears when he is approaching from some far away hill, yet how he grows bigger and bigger and his torch ever-brighter as he draws near. The whole camp had been silent, listening and contemplating the paradigm-shifting lecture, except for her own toddler, Klengah, who let out with occasional, rebellious yawns and squawks. She wanted her mama to shut up and come lie beside her and Papa to sleep. It was growing quite late, and the tribe members always rose early, so they could get most of their daily trek done before the heat of the noon day sun. Klaarongah gestured a sweet goodnight to the crowd and gave a few hugs to some of them, before trotting over to her little daughter, who promptly darted out into the cold from beneath her Papa's huge feathery-blanket of wings, and into her mama's arms. Within a few minutes Klengah was sound asleep.

A couple of young hunters had volunteered to take turns watching over the tribe while the rest of them slept. Having evolved on their dangerous world Kaarp, where something could always be lurking in the tall grasses of the savannahs or thick reeds of the marshes, both Klaarongah and Krawwgh could remain sensually aware of their surroundings, while still achieving a recuperative rest. Except for the usual sounds of the camp—crackling from the toasty campfire and the rustlings and snoring of the sleeping tribe—it was quiet.

Arriving just outside the camp and hiding behind yet another of the areas ubiquitous sandstone spires, Mntangua had followed in the shadow of the tribe, all the way since their departure from home camp, three days earlier. He had listened to most of Klaarongah's lecture with both amusement and disdain. Shivering under his old, torn, and filthy blanket, he watched them all with hateful envy, as he schemed about how he would extract his revenge once they reached the beaches. His stealthy vigilance had been disturbed by the lingering aromas from the earlier roasted meat, making it difficult for him to think about anything else. Still, he'd stoically push his gnawing hunger from the forefront of his mind and patiently wait a few more hours until everybody was sound asleep. Then, he'd sneak into the camp and devour whatever scraps he could find. So he waited and then waited some more.

He wasn't the only one waiting. A pride of lions had settled in a couple of miles away and two lionesses had set out to go night hunting. They too, had been attracted by the delicious aromas and noises of the camp, and had been waiting a long time just for the chance to pounce on somebody. As it turned out, that somebody was going to be HIM! One lioness had silently scaled to the top of the very same sandstone formation he was hiding behind and squatted in a pounce position, while the other crept up to a nearby thicket of tall grass, ready to help hunt and give chase if need be. With near simultaneity, they struck. He screamed as over 200 pounds of ferocity fell down on him. Massive claws clutched his scrawny body and huge canines sank deep into each thigh. He cried out in agony and passed out. He was completely helpless, as they dragged him back into the thicket. And when he came to, he saw her, that same damn devil-bird at the heart of all his misery!

Klaarongah and Krawwgh had heard everything. While he gathered up their sleeping daughter, she thundered over to the commotion on the camp's dark side. Startled, one of the lionesses let go of Mntangua's legs and pounced at Klaarongah. With more agility than a professional bantam weight boxer, Klaarongah pivoted and batted the lion off to one side, then instantly pinned her under one of her giant talons and immobilized her. Then, Klaarongah raised her huge dagger-tipped beak skyward and arched it downward into the lion's side with incredible force, caving in the ribcage and severing its heart. The other lioness had tried to bite at one of Klaarongah's legs, but missed. Klaarongah pivoted and delivered a powerful front kick that knocked that lioness on her back and sent her scrambling into the darkness.

Klaarongah picked up Mntangua's unconscious and hemorrhaging body and sprinted back to Krawwgh and the camp. She gently laid him down on a mat that Krawwgh had set out, while one of the young camp guards offered up his tunic to shred and use for tourniquets. With some sticks from the campfire supply, Klaarongah twisted and tightened the cloth band until it stopped the hemorrhaging and then set up continuous monitoring of his vital signs. Watching her carefully, the guard did the same on the less wounded leg. Krawwgh pulled out their emergency medical supply box and flung it over to Klaarongah. She opened it and retrieved a tube of their pan-spectrum anti-microbial jell, a can of their wound sterilizing and cauterizing cream, and a spool of their wound-fusing, healing bandages. She took a syringe of hydrogen peroxide to flush out any debris from the deep-puncture and bone-crushing wound, then applied a combination of the anti-microbial and sterilizer and wrapped the no longer bleeding wound with special bandages. They had done all that they could for Mntangua. Now, all that was left was to wait and see. Krawwgh handed their snoozing toddler over to Klaarongah and nestled down by Mntangua's side, where he would watch over their patient until morning.

Only a few hours later, and the camp was already beginning to stir. Mntangua was still unconscious, but his vital signs looked encouraging. Krawwgh and Klaarongah discussed his situation. He would surely die a horrible death if he was left alone and unattended, and though it broke her heart not to be with little Klengah to witness her first ever experiences at the beach, she knew that, because of her dexterous hands, she would be much more able to look after Mntangua than Krawwgh. She lovingly hugged, nuzzled, and eye-kissed Klengah goodbye, while Krawwgh gave her a great big bag of cool water, some of the necessary medical supplies, and nearly all of their dried meat, since they would soon be able to feed themselves on the ocean's revived bounty. He enfolded his loving mate in another winged embrace and eye-kissed her 'goodbye.' Krawwgh then turned to face the tribe, which was hastily loading up their belligerent and bellowing camels with their heavy packs of gear, preparing to depart. Over a shoulder he gave his lover a last, loving glance, grabbed up a bag of supplies in his big beak, enfolded his squawking and protesting daughter in his powerful talons, and leaped into the sky.

Feeling the furious winds generated by Krawwgh's departure, Mntangua coughed and sputtered as he came to. Through his bleary vision and light-headedness, he squinted as he struggled to focus. Then, Klaarongah's intimidating features came into view. Right then he wanted to rise to his feet and run, but he could not move at all, except to lift his head. "W-what happened? He rasped. "W-why are YOU here?" He set his head back down on the make-shift pillow in utter exhaustion. Even though she felt no personal affection toward the superstitious fool, she did feel sorry for him. He was in a pathetic state, both physically and mentally. She quickly put her helmet back on, so that he would be able to understand any replies to his questions or statements, then gently scooped up his head and gave him a couple of sips of water. He slurped, swallowed, sputtered, and coughed at the splendid relief of its soothing coolness. She laid his head back down and then stood up, towering over him as she dance-explained all the events of the previous evening. As his memories came flooding back, so, too, did the terror as Mntangua remembered that he had been dragged by the lions back into the high grass to be eaten alive. And it was her, ONE

OF THE EVIL BIRD-GODS, who had saved him from a gruesome death. "So it was YOU who saved me?" Klaarongah nodded her head. He feebly pointed to the water bag, and she tenderly scooped up his head again and helped him sip some more. After swallowing, his voice was stronger. "Why…why did you save me?"

Once again, rising to her intimidating full height Klaarongah explained. "Because you needed it. No sentient being should have to endure such a gruesome death, not even an OUTCAST!"

Mntangua suddenly seized in agony. His massively wounded thigh was sending racking waves of pain to his brain. Quickly rechecking his vitals, Klaarongah noted that his temperature had soared to 102 degrees, while his blood pressure was dropping. After a few sniffs of his wounded leg, she knew what had to be done. Sadly, the leg was dying. Too much damage had occurred to the bone and blood vessels within. It was gangrenous. It had healed well on the outside, but now it was too infected to heal from within. He would go into shock and die unless she amputated. She poked an anesthetic pill into his mouth, and within a couple of seconds, he was unconscious. She stripped him naked and thoroughly washed him down with hydrogen peroxide, but she couldn't take the time to shave or surgically prepare him further. These were far less than ideal conditions for performing a surgery like those she'd have back at the life pod, but she'd make the best of it and do her utmost, regardless. She took the tube of the pan-spectrum, anti-microbial, and liberally coated her hands, forelimbs, and all the edges and surfaces of her beak. Then, she opened wide and put several large dollops on her tongue. Like all birds, she didn't produce any saliva, so she had to flex and coil her tubular tongue many times to thoroughly coat all the surfaces of her inner beak and throat. She was now ready; she grabbed the severely punctured and partially crushed limb and placed it firmly in her gaping maw a few inches above the wound. She slowly bit down with a gradually increasing but even pressure until she had severed it completely off! Naturally, Mntangua began hemorrhaging again, so Klaarongah took some more of the anti-microbial and rubbed it on the bleeding stump. Then, she took the wound sterilizer and cauterizer and elevated the stump while she liberally coated it. In less than ten seconds, the stump stopped bleeding, and the patient had lost little blood—especially for an amputation. She finished the surgery by applying the wound-fusing bandages.

Convinced that her patient was safe and holding steady, she washed and cleaned him up, as well as his bed, and then herself. Klaargh then took in a big beak, full of water, but did not swallow. Instead, she swirled it around as best she could in order to rinse the extremely bitter anti-microbial solution from her oral cavity. She repeated this procedure twice more to ensure she had rid herself of all of it. Given the remoteness of the location and the lack of normal surgical support gear and personnel, Mntangua was very lucky to have such a willing and capable surgeon and nurse at his side. All she could do now was to continue looking after him and wait to see whether or not he recovered. After that, if he could learn to reject his religiously inspired paranoia, maybe 'someone' would petition the tribal elders on his behalf for a reunion with the tribe!

By early afternoon the next day, the tribe had made it to the Somali shoreline. As always, Krawwgh had flown on ahead with Klengah still safely tucked within his talons. Together, they rode the rising thermals of the heat-driven air and glided in gentle arcs and dives. Now, Klengah enjoyed every moment up in the sky with her big papa and continued flapping her little forelimbs and striding with her dangling, spindly legs. Meanwhile, the cool, shore-lapping waves offered splendid relief to the hot and exhausted desert nomads, who were hurriedly stripping on the beach and diving into its surf.

XXIII. On the Beach

First, making sure that Klengah had instinctively extended her legs and flexed her knees in a practiced anticipation of landing, Krawwgh and Klengah set down on the sandy beach, and he released her from his mighty grip. He watched with fatherly pride and cautious curiosity, as his darling toddler charged up to the in-rushing waves and thrilled at the delightful coolness enveloping her talons. As enticing as the waves were, she was afraid to venture any farther, despite the beckoning encouragement from all her tribe mates. That's when her big daddy stealthily waddled up behind her and dove his big beak between her legs and lifted his startled daughter up until she was sitting on his head. Next, he tilted his beak skyward, forcing Klengah to cling tightly and shimmy down his thick neck until her bottom was comfortably balanced on his broad, muscular shoulders. He waddled out into the surf as Klengah fearfully squawked while clinging tightly to Krawwgh's neck feathers. He folded in his talons, as the waves lifted him and his puzzled daughter, and they continued floating toward their friends who gently patted and rubbed them both, while admiring the oily smoothness of their wet feathers.

Slowly, Klengah was settling down and gaining confidence, and she was fascinated to see all the children bobbing, laughing, and frolicking about in the surf. She let go of Krawwgh and plunged head first into the ocean then quickly ascended. SHE LOVED IT, and joyously squawked and bragged about her new feat. As she instinctively folded her long neck back against the top of her body, then tucked her beak down while also folding in her talons, she discovered she was buoyant, too, and enjoyed the languid sensation of floating and bobbing on the waves. She turned to proudly show her papa when she saw him unfurl his huge wings, extend his short neck and immerse himself completely in the waves. He repeated this several times, luxuriating in the ocean's watery coolness while also gulping up beaks full of delicious, salty brine, just as he and all his fellow krrugh often did during his childhood in planet Kaarp's salty polar oceans.

All the play was making them hungry, so several tribe members unfolded the fishing nets, unpacked their bows and spears, and began fishing for dinner. Other adults and teens got busy setting up tents, tarps, and starting the campfire. After leaving his elated but exhausted daughter with Nbegwe and her baby, Ndula, Krawwgh returned to the surf and helped fish for dinner. It wasn't very long before the fishermen—aided with their big nets, and Krawwgh's lightening reflexes—were hauling in a sizeable catch, and by nightfall, they had more than enough to feed the entire tribe for a couple of days. Krawwgh had devoured a couple of pikes and gars and swallowed up some delicious seaweed as well, to hold him over as he waddled up to Nbegwe's tent. Thoughtfully remaining outside, he shook himself furiously several times until he was dry, then dropped a couple of big fish at Nbegwe's feet. He put his helmet back on and politely asked Nbegwe if she would please look after Klengah for a couple of nights while he left to bring Klaarongah back. Nbegwe responded that she would be honored and that he need not worry. Truly grateful, Krawwgh enfolded Nbegwe in a winged embrace and gave Klengah an eye-kiss goodbye.

Like every loving parent, Krawwgh hated to hear his daughter squawking in distress as he left, but he took comfort in knowing just how happy she'd be, when he returned with her mother. As he hurtled back toward Klaarongah, he reflected on all the death they had rained down on humanity and how these people—their trusted and beloved tribe—were only spared by the drones because of their precarious proximity to the ostriches, and how much more isolated and lonely they would have been now, if these people hadn't been spared. Then, he mused about how much surer the future of any of their offspring would be if he could breed with these comparatively brainy beings instead. He knew that could never happen, however, because krrughs and humans were entirely incompatible, genetically and physically, and as all their brightest biologists and geneticists knew over six decades earlier, the closest genomes to their own were in fact, the ostriches—those very same feral, primitive, and barely sentient beings that they had succeeded in cross-fertilizing only once, producing Klengah—their adorable but mentally stunted daughter. He knew what was waiting for him when they returned from their summer hiatus. Immediately, he shoved the humiliating deeds and gnawing uncertainties from his mind and instead, concentrated on reaching his lover and the patient—if he was still alive. He was ecstatic when he began receiving her over his helmet.

Soon, they were reunited and entangled in an amorous love-dance and groping embrace. Because of their earlier duty-imposed abstinence in order to save all their juices for all the breeding attempts and species sparing copulations and then Klaarongah's delicate pregnancy, they hadn't been together in months. They lustfully mated until they were exhausted. Meanwhile, Mntangua peacefully slumbered away. As they cuddled afterwards, Klaarongah told Krawwgh all about her surgery on the shocked patient, and then they both wondered how the old human would cope when he awoke to discover his new stump. Sensing Klaarongah's hunger, Krawwgh graciously regurgitated up some of his seafood dinner for her to relish. Afterwards, he delighted in telling her about some—but not all—of Klengah's exploits upon encountering the beach and ocean. Then, he waxed on about how big the moon was and how it's bright reflection shimmered and rippled on the black waves of the night sea.

With a sudden groan and raspy cough, Mntangua began to stir. Still groggy from the powerful anesthetic, he peered with his blurry vision and saw his loyal nurse and her mate sitting down by his foot. ONE FOOT? Wait, what had happened to the other? Panicking, he felt around under his blanket made from a black plastic bag, when it finally dawned on him. ONE OF HIS LEGS WAS GONE! "What-what did you do with my leg?" He screamed. Klaarongah gently eased him back down under the blanket, then gave him some water. Krawwgh fetched his helmet and stood up to tell him that his leg's removal was absolutely necessary in order to save his life because it had become gangrenous. With tears streaming down his face, Mntangua sputtered, "You should have let me die!" Then, he painfully turned on his side, no longer facing them, and began crying.

This was truly strange behavior from Klaarongah and Krawwgh's perspective, because on their world, anyone having their life saved felt truly lucky and eternally grateful to any and all beings involved on their behalf, regardless of the injury. Back on Kaarp, everyone mattered, and you could always count on help from anyone around you all the time. "How tragically alone and helpless these humans must often feel," Klaarongah said. Krawwgh agreed. It was growing late, and they were getting hungry again, so Krawwgh took to the air once more, in search of a quick dinner. He returned in less than an hour, with two prairie voles and a large rat. Klaarongah retrieved the infrared laser cannon from one of their storage bags and began irradiating a nearby flat top rock, making it hot enough to cook on. Having watched many of her human tribal members prepare their meals, she knew what to do for her patient's dietary needs. Meanwhile, she and Krawwgh enjoyed the aromas while chomping and swallowing their raw morsels.

Even after crying himself to sleep, Mntangua began to stir again. The aromas must have become unbearable to resist since he hadn't eaten in three days. Klaarongah gave him a small thigh, and he tore into it. This was a good sign that he was recuperating and willing to go on living, if he accepted food from someone he did not trust. They all sat there in silence, devouring their meals. They exchanged glances while the flames of Krawwgh's hastily assembled campfire illuminated their expressionless features, as it crackled and flickered against the starry black sky.

Finally sated, Mntangua painfully rose to a sitting position on his sleeping bag and started right in criticizing Klaarongah for having saved his wretched life. She put her helmet back on so that she would be able to respond. "Now that I'm an outcast from my 'beloved' tribe and incidentally, all the people left on Earth, what good was any of this?" he demanded.

Klaarongah danced in response. "If you continue to heal and start to trust us—not worship, but just trust—we will help you walk again, and when we arrive at the beach, we will petition the tribal elders to let you rejoin the tribe."

Mntangua was floored by the first hopeful thoughts he'd had in months. Even with these gracious offers, however, his distrusting and cynical nature kicked in immediately, as he fired off more accusations. "You're the reason I was discarded like trash in the first place, why should I trust you now?" At this point Krawwgh joined the conversation.

"Although you may think of us as impartial, cruel, and genocidal murderers, we are quite capable of love and compassion and can empathize with anyone's suffering, even former enemies. We took no joy in the annihilation of nearly all your species, but our scholars had studied your numerous and varied cultures for decades, and they knew there would be no collective will to ever stop your vicious wars, nor cease the flagrant disregard you had shown towards your fellow creatures and your planet's precious ecology."

Finally getting around to answering Mntangua's question, Krawwgh said. "You should trust us because no one else cares. If you'll remember, it was the tribe that so angrily spurned you, not us." Krawwgh continued. "We were very upset that you snuck onboard our vessel, especially since we had known of your distrust in us for quite some time and worried about you instigating rebellion or sabotage. But it was the elders who were most angered by the trespass, and it was they who decided to expel you."

Still angry, Mntangua continued his accusations. "They do all this because you are gods, and they fear your wrath. Why didn't you intervene on my behalf earlier?"

Klaarongah answered. "We told you when we first met with all the tribe that we only wanted to live among you in peace, not interfere with your day-to-day lives. And we knew how important it was for the tribe to draft and enforce its own moral codes and laws to govern itself. You became an outcast because you violated their interpretation of the rules and because of your demeanor toward us."

"But you are gods, why…?"

Krawwgh interrupted him. "You say we are gods, yet you willingly violated our home and accused us of horrible transgressions. Why?" At that, Mntangua fell silent. For the first time, he realized that his reasoning was incomplete.

Then, Klaarongah questioned him. "If we are gods or demons, why don't you fear us as much as the others supposedly do?"

Mntangua looked embarrassed. "I d-don't know. It's just a feeling, I guess." Klaarongah gave a questioning but knowing look to Krawwgh, who nodded. So Klaarongah started rattling off things Mntangua might have seen or misunderstood. "Perhaps, you suspect we are not gods because you've seen my mate eat your dead enemies, or caught us excreting, just like all animals do, and that we don't have any temples for you to worship us, nor do we ask the tribe to perform ceremonies in our honor!"

Upon hearing that, Mntangua's face went completely blank, as fears of divine retribution rushed in. What she revealed next floored him.

"The truth is, dear Mntangua, WE ARE NOT GODS OR DEMONS, and we don't possess any magical or supernatural powers, either! Just as you humans were the cleverest beings on your world, we birds are the cleverest on ours, and we have learned so much about nature that we can do things that might seem unnatural and, thus appears magical or supernatural. But in all that we have seen and learned as we explored our universe, we find no evidence for magic, mysticism, or the supernatural, and, thus, NO REASON to believe in gods.

"Given enough time and patience, guided by rational skepticism and the methods of good science, ALL THINGS ARE POTENTIALLY KNOWABLE even if not fully understandable.

"And a rational inquiry into things is always superior to a mystical testimony in finding the truth! If miracles are unnecessary, so, too, ARE GODS!"

After pausing in silence for a couple of minutes to give Mntangua the chance to comprehend and digest all that they had revealed, Klaarongah continued. "You see, dear Mntangua, you were not punished because of your doubts about us, but rather because of your trespass and desire for rebellion against us." Mntangua was rapt in attention, as Klaarongah went still further. "We will reveal these same truths to the rest of the tribe as soon as they further learn and develop their reasoning abilities and critical problem-solving skills. Then, they will discover that they no longer need to live in fear of divine retribution, or spend their days preparing for eternal life." Mntangua's eyes grew big as his previous mystical and religious beliefs were coming under reasoned attacks by beings much more intelligent than himself.

For the first time in his long life, Mntangua felt the restless 'fight within himself' ease. Their sound reasoning was better than anything he had ever heard in his life, and that they were willing to forgive him and help him get back in his tribe, was more than he could have possibly expected from them.

He reached out to Klaarongah and tearfully hugged her. "Thank you for all you've done for me. Yes, I will gladly go with you to camp!" She gently squeezed him back, greatly relieved in his change of mind. From here on out, she would dedicate her efforts to help him relearn to walk and then rejoin the tribe. After their goodnight hugs, Mntangua was soon peacefully asleep.

They all arose early the next morning and began planning his therapy. After a quick breakfast, Krawwgh sifted through the fire's wood pile and found two sticks long and strong enough to serve as crutches. He gave them to Mntangua and Klaarongah. Then, she asked him to rise. Slowly, painfully he did so, and nestled the Y-shaped ends underneath his armpits. While standing on his one leg, he balanced and then shifted the ends of his two crutches out in front of himself. Next, he sprung off his foot and hopped forward. It was somewhat uncomfortable, but manageable, and after practicing for several minutes, he got smoother and better balanced with each step, only falling a few times in the process. It took a lot more effort than regular two-legged walking and made his arms tired and a little sore, but he was confident that he would get accustomed to them in due time. Anyway, he was now mobile again and able to join them as they began their trek to the beach.

As always, Krawwgh flew on ahead and surveyed all he could see in his big circles, while Klaarongah patiently straggled along with Mntangua. When the pain and fatigue became too much, she would squat down and tell him to hop on and hug her neck. Then, she would break into a gentle trot, with her patient safely riding along. He wasn't much heavier than Klengah, who frequently rode along on Klaarongah's broad back, but she knew that in his weakened condition, he would likely fall from his high perch unless she maintained a slow, smooth pace with frequent stops for him to rest or relieve himself.

While mounted on top of Klaarongah, Mntangua fell into short snoozes as he painfully revisited those hateful thoughts and suspicions he had against these two beings, who now struggled in earnest to look after him and bring him back to the tribe. His eyes teared up with shame, as he now realized what all the others had known all along, that Klaarongah and Krawwgh were truly GOOD—better really, than anyone he had ever known.

Nightfall soon set, and they decided to stop for the evening and settle down. Mntangua opened his crude bedding, while Klaarongah got busy, scrounging up sticks and scrub-bush for a fire, and Krawwgh took off to hunt for dinner. About an hour later, Krawwgh had returned with a small dear carcass. He quickly bit off the head and hooves and tore it apart, down the middle. Then, he chomped down and bit off one of the meaty thighs to hold him over until Klaarongah could join them. As Mntangua sat there, watching the ghastly display of Krawwgh crunching on bones and shredding up tough muscles and sinews, he was fascinated by the display of raw power and realized this had convinced him and the tribe of the duo's physical superiority. When coupled with their tremendous knowledge and technical accomplishments, it was small wonder they thought these two were gods. Soon, Klaarongah had joined them and graciously offered Mntangua his cooked share of the deer. He thanked them both, and they finished their meals.

Both Klaarongah and Krawwgh were still helmeted, so Mntangua started to question them about the krrugh and planet Kaarp. Since he was farther along in the meal than Klaarongah, Krawwgh responded and began describing their world, the krrugh, and all their fellow creatures. Mntangua felt truly sad for them when Krawwgh explained how they had been selected to take the trip, knowing that they would never see their families, friends, or any fellow beings again. But his mood brightened, when Krawwgh explained what honor had been bestowed upon Klaarongah and him, to take the mission to Earth. Then, Krawwgh told Mntangua about all the features of Kaarp, it's huge and desolate deserts with their tiny and distant oases, and how the krrugh evolved to hunt the large and dangerous klacks and gucks in the tall grasses of the savannahs. And how in ages long past, they all congregated at the salt marshes each breeding season, where they were preyed upon by swarms of flies, giant ocean crocodiles, and camouflaged amphibious snakes, as they nested their precious eggs. Then, he waxed on, telling Mntangua about Kaarp's glorious and frequent dawns and sunsets that captioned its short days. But he ended the conversation by saying that Earth was a more hospitable world, with far more beauty and diversity.

Somewhat timidly, Mntangua asked whether or not he and Klaarongah had been successful in completing their mission objectives. Krawwgh paused to think, before answering. "Yes, but only in part."

Since they had very effectively eliminated the Earth's primary cause of pollution, remediated the atmosphere and hydrosphere, and saved untold numbers of species from a man-made extinction, Earth was rebounding back and regaining its natural ecological balance. As for the other part of their mission, things were not going well. They had succeeded in producing only one, viable offspring, despite all their advanced genetic tinkering and animal husbandry. Knowing how limited Mntangua's science knowledge was, Krawwgh kept things simple by explaining to him that despite their frequent attempts to mate with the ostriches, they had only one child—their daughter, Klengah. Krawwgh didn't feel it was necessary to reveal that she would never be smart like her parents, and that he would have to continue mating with ostriches when the tribe returned to their home hunting grounds, in the fall.

A sudden surge of post-surgical pain overwhelmed Mntangua, and Krawwgh called out for Klaarongah, who had taken leave of them to relieve herself. Already anticipating her patient's agony, she trotted over to them with the emergency medical kit, reached within and retrieved a powerful analgesic. She deftly placed it on Mntangua's tongue, and then gave him some water to wash it down. Lying back out on his bag-blanket, he thanked them both and soon fell soundly asleep, no doubt, exhausted from his pain and the previous exertions of the day. Tomorrow would only be more of the same as they drew nearer to the beach.

Back at the beach camp, things were progressing smoothly. The entire tribe was rejoicing in the relieving sea breezes, salt air, and bountiful seafood. The men had to only caste their nets once every couple of days to feed the tribe. Meanwhile, Nbegwe and some of the other trained mothers continued teaching all the other women, children, and men. They passed on all the wisdom and knowledge Klaarongah and Krawwgh had bestowed upon them. There was much to learn about being a new and improved human that struggled to learn and then practice lessons on empathy, conflict resolution, and diplomacy towards others. This was in addition to the more standard curriculum of reading, writing, math, science, and history. All the adults and teenagers received hygiene and health training, too, including birth control and pregnancy, STD prevention, population control measures, and economics as it related to the tribe's bartering practices. In all they did within the tribe, Klaarongah and Krawwgh cautioned them against repeating the dreadful mistakes of all the former people who once shared their world. This tribe would be different and better, as they were patiently supported and strongly encouraged to learn and use the new lessons Klaarongah and Krawwgh taught them. Then, all these teachings would be handed down to guide future generations in perpetuity.

By early afternoon, school adjourned, and the students swarmed to the beach where Klengah would be waiting to greet and play with them. It seemed that with each passing hour, she was growing bigger and stronger, while also beginning to display some of her instinctive krrugh terror bird nature. This became evident one evening when a large and deadly king cobra snake slithered into camp. As frightened mothers gathered up their children, and some of the men went scrambling for their weapons, Klengah pranced up toward the snake and began circling around and darting in and out. Nbegwe was mortified with fear and shame, and cried while watching her entrusted charge engage the lethal creature. First, the snake spat a stream of venom aimed for Klengah's eyes. But she dodged the deadly spray. Then, the cobra lunged toward Klengah but missed again. She easily side-stepped the motion and then pounced with lightning speed and pinned down and immobilized its coiling body. Then, she bit its head off! First shocked but then overjoyed, Nbegwe rushed over to check Klengah and see if she had been bitten, during the deadly encounter. She hadn't, but enjoyed the concerned hugs and kisses regardless. Nbegwe and numerous others gathered around the proud peacock to thank her for her brave protection. Whatever her intellectual limitations were, it was clear that even at her young age, she was more than able to defend herself and her tribe.

This display of power and savagery might have made some of her tribe fearful, or make them act cautiously when she was near—perhaps even pulling their little children away. But she was completely unchanged by the event and remained as gentle, engaging, and playful as before. She seemed to understand that she had to be very slow and gentle around babies and toddlers, yet was now strong enough to engage in short sprints with bigger kids on her back or grapple with some of the oldest boys on the hot sandy beach. Despite all the joys and adventures of the day, she'd spend a couple of hours each evening, anxiously pacing back and forth at the camp's periphery, cawing out to her missing parents. Nbegwe was truly touched to witness this. She could readily empathize and imagine how lonely she'd feel to be separated from her daughter and sister, even if only for a couple of nights.

XXIV. Judgment

The next afternoon, Krawwgh was happily flying over and shadowing the camp. Many ran out from their tarps and tents to shade once again underneath his huge silhouette as he honked and cawed to his beloved people. Klengah was positively ecstatic as she jumped, cawed, and squawked impatiently for her big papa to land. She ran up to him the second he landed, and he enfolded her in his crushing feathery embrace. She was already a foot taller than him, but that mattered to neither as she coiled her long neck down to nuzzle and eye-kiss her papa. Just then, she heard another honk and low caw and eagerly slipped from Krawwgh's embrace and sprinted out to see her mama. Klaarongah was thrilled to see her sprinting so fast and startled at how much she had grown in only a couple of days. She squatted down to let a very thankful Mntangua glide off her back and then handed him his crutches to stand with. She stood back up and reached out for her daughter, and Klengah jumped up into her waiting arms. They nuzzled their beaks and eye-kissed for what seemed like an eternity, before Klaarongah put her back down.

Like any unsure youngster, Klengah cowered behind her big mama when she suddenly noticed the stranger off to her mother's side. He was small, crumpled, whitish, and wrinkly—not at all like her youthful companions—and he sported long tree limbs for arms and had only one talon to stand on. He was different from all the others in the camp. Even though she sensed her daughter's distress, Klaarongah took her by the hand and slowly approached Mntangua, while Klengah squawked in protest. Klaarongah gently stroked her frightened daughter as she reached for Mntangua's hand. He understood the situation and dropped his crutches and balanced himself against Klaarongah's mighty arm. Now, Klengah could see that he was just another man and his 'tree limbs' were something other than his arms that he needed to hop about. She came out from beneath her mama's arm and then gently reached out to hug Mntangua. Overwhelmed by the display of trust and affection, and flooded with shame for having ever contemplated killing such a gentle and trusting being, Mntangua burst out in tears and muffled his sobs against Klengah's shoulder. She never let go, as he continued his crying. Finally, he lifted his face to hers, and she gave him a gentle eye-kiss, then licked his salty tears from the side of her beak. Klaarongah was moved by seeing how gentle and loving her darling daughter was. She stooped back down to hand Mntangua his crutches, and the trio approached the gathering crowd. Krawwgh had already greeted many of them, and he made sure to hug and thank Nbegwe for looking after their daughter. Then, it was Klaarongah's turn to thank Nbegwe for the crucial babysit.

Gently cradling little Ndula, Klaarongah then asked Nbegwe for yet another favor. Gesturing toward the grizzled little old man standing on crutches next to Klengah, Klaarongah asked Nbegwe to assemble another meeting with the tribal elders to see if they would reconsider Mntangua's case, and allow him to rejoin the tribe. She explained that she thought he had changed his ways and was now a more humble and inclusive man, far less likely to ever stir up any trouble. She made it clear to her, however, that the decision was theirs alone to make, and that she and Krawwgh would abide by and enforce, whatever the elders decided. Nbegwe said she would convene a meeting immediately, as she scurried through the large crowd, yelling for the other tribal elders.

Soon, there was a gathering of ten members off to one side of the much larger crowd. As they all crouched there, squatting on their heels, they discussed his situation. Mntangua waited nervously for their ruling. His gaze was lowered in a fearful, obedient submission. Whatever the final verdict was, he knew how much he owed Klaarongah and Krawwgh for looking after and believing in him, and he would respect the decision, regardless. All the while Klengah had remained at his side, patiently patting and stroking him with her little three-fingered hand in an attempt to soothe him, somehow. The group of noble elders dispersed, and Nbegwe slowly approached Mntangua. At first, her manner of speech was very formal and austere, and Mntangua could barely look her in the eye after remembering his dismissive attitude toward her, in the many months past. Now, he was here, trembling fearfully, as he awaited HER delivery of the counsel's judgment. He thought he was going to pass out from all the tension, when he saw her little round face break into a big, beautiful smile. Then, she gathered him up in a loving embrace! Soon, the entire tribe swarmed around him as they hugged, kissed, and back-slapped Mntangua, signifying his acceptance back into this tribe of new and improved humans.

He wanted to run over and hug Klaarongah for all she had done for him, but couldn't because he was surrounded by all the tribe's children, women, and his band of former hunt-buddies. Instead, he waved 'thank you' to her and then blew her a kiss. She did a hand-to-beak gesture back at him in reply, then cuddled her youngster up next to her. After a celebratory feast for Klaarongah's and Krawwgh's safe return—which now included old Mntangua's reunion with the tribe—the camp settled down for the evening buffeted by cool and gentle sea breezes under a big bright moon. Mntangua was just getting settled into the first real bed he'd slept in, in months, when he suddenly realized he had a companion! Klengah squatted down and nestled right next to him and then gently laid her head in his lap. Mntangua let loose with a big guffaw and threw an arm around his new buddy. Soon, they drifted off on a dream together.

XXV. Conclusion

Klaarongah, Krawwgh, and Klengah spent the rest of that summer and many more thereafter, down on the pleasant Somali beaches with all their beloved tribe. With time, Klaarongah and Krawwgh reminisced less about their home world, Kaarp, and all their loved ones left behind and grew evermore enchanted with Earth and its people. As that precious first summer at the beach drew to a close, they became even closer as a tribe when Klaarongah and Krawwgh revealed, as promised to Mntangua, that they were not gods at all, but mere mortals like the rest of them, born into the world to live, love, and eventually die. In all their world's investigations into nature—from the tiniest sub-atomic particles to the incredible vastness of outer space—they had never encountered evidence of supernatural beings or paranormal powers, things, and events. These things weren't necessary at all to live worthwhile lives, or create a moral and just society. Nor was it necessary to fear anything or anyone after death, which was a natural and inevitable result for all living things.

Rather, they urged them to live in the here and now, with open but rationally skeptical minds, respectful of their elders and the things they accomplished in the past, but living in the moment while preparing a better world for future generations. If anything was to survive an individual's life, it was the memories and reputation she formed while she lived with all the others around her. The goal was to enjoy life, but to live it in an honorable fashion. When they returned back to the life pod that fall, Klaarongah and Krawwgh decided that the secrecy and lethal protection were no longer necessary, and so, they permanently shut down the vessel's defenses. Then, they invited ALL tribal members to join them inside, and even began teaching some classes within its strange walls. There they would continue to teach and train their beloved Earth family, always emphasizing the best reasoning and attitudes to assure continued peace between one another and harmony with nature. This would set this new type of mankind on a much better course for a long and worthwhile future.

Since Krawwgh and Klaarongah were now back in their home and had access to all its laboratories and stores of knowledge, they got busy right away, cloning some tissue from Mntangua in order to create and then surgically graft a new leg onto him. It worked very well, and proved strong and agile enough for him to play with his new best buddy, Klengah. She continued growing bigger and stronger with each passing day, and would soon reach sexual maturity. Then, it would be time for her parents to introduce her to some new friends, the ostriches. They could tell she missed the beaches. They all did. But school had started back up for the mothers and children, and now that they were allowed to board the life pod, every day was turning into a special occasion with so much to see, learn, and ponder. Once the lessons ended, however, Klengah was surrounded with all her tribal family—playing, cuddling, and enjoying many precious moments together.

Finally, it was ostrich breeding season again and as before, Krawwgh had already been storing up as much of his semen as possible, by a self-imposed abstinence. He truly ached for Klaarongah and hated their time apart this way, but she was always understanding. They desperately hoped that their continued efforts and sufferings would eventually result in some sisters and brothers for Klengah, as well as the continuation of their race. And so they started out together again, but this time with their daughter in tow. Klengah was now too big for her papa to fly very far with, so after she saw Klaarongah and Krawwgh join up and hop-glide into the distance a couple of times as she sprinted to catch up, she gave it a try. After a few jarring landings, from Krawwgh's powerful lifts, she got the hang of it and began smoothly hopping with big jumps, just like her mama always did.

Soon, Krawwgh and Klengah were in range of a large group of ostriches with several adult males and females. There weren't any tall grasses to dive into and hide nearby, but there was a big hill about a half a mile from the flock. Klengah was startled to see these other big birds so much like her and her mama, and she started squawking excitedly at them. Krawwgh then gently silenced her, and they hid behind the hill. Just then, Klaarongah caught up with them and took over, soothing

Klengah, as Krawwgh put on his male ostrich costume again. Klengah continued squirming and kicking in startled protest as Klaarongah gently, but firmly, restrained her while Krawwgh hustled over to the group on his stilted artificial ostrich legs. Reviewing in his mind the typical male ostrich sparring and mating behaviors, he decided that, this time, he would try the alpha male role and subdue his fellow suitors. Sure enough, a large male not previously encountered ran up to challenge him. Krawwgh was more than ready, as he began kicking his ostrich stilts and batting his huge wings at the befuddled and easily overwhelmed opponent. After a few brief moments, the rattled, but okay, ostrich retreated from the battle. The other males had apparently sensed Krawwgh's determination and retreated to the periphery of the big flock as well.

Krawwgh was quite pleased and wasted no time starting his articulated, long-necked, costume head swoons, and his recording of ritual mating throat booms. Soon, a trio of females squatted and assumed the position for mating. He immediately slid up behind the closest one and began working his penile syringes of engineered sperm cells. He repeated the deed, twice more with the other two, trying as always to increase the probability that at least one of them would conceive. He was just finishing up with the last one, when something large, and slightly askew, caught his attention. It was Klengah, who proudly pranced up to some of the disinterested females and juveniles. Klaarongah had apparently tired of restraining and muting her any longer and decided that now was as good a time as any, for her daughter to get fully acquainted with these new beings and hopeful future suitors. Krawwgh agreed, now that he was done with his duty, and so he sat by and watched their daughter. Despite her noisy squawks and formidable size, they barely seemed to notice her, which caused her increasing distress. She started poking them gently with her big and unusual beak, while simultaneously stroking and patting them with her hands, in a desperate gambit for attention. Both Klaarongah and Krawwgh were acutely alert and ready to intervene if, in her agitated state, she should start any of her powerful kicks or lethal down-thrusting stabs, as she was already more powerful than any ostrich. Her parents were not the only ones noticing her disturbances, however. That same big male that Krawwgh had so thoroughly trounced earlier, was sizing her up. It must have been truly confounding for this male ostrich, as he grew near and caught her female scent, yet noticed her much bigger physique and strange beak. Since Klengah didn't know any better, she didn't try to crouch and hide her size, or mimic any ostrich behavior. Instead, she just stood there and stared at the approaching male, as he circled his long neck and started his sonata of throat booms. She continued to watch with a detached amusement, as he kept up his repertoire. He even pecked at the ground—ordering her submission—in growing sexual frustration.

But when he came up behind her and tried to force her down, she scurried ahead and quickly turned to face him. He tried again, and this time, her rebuff was even more severe. She slapped him with the side of her beak, and then chastised him with several head-shakes and beak chatter-clacks. At this point, it looked like Klengah had had enough for one day, and there was always tomorrow for another try. By then, a female ostrich had caught the frustrated male's attention, and he was off in a flash for an easier conquest. Klaarongah thundered out from behind the hill and cawed to Klengah, who promptly sprinted back to her mother as her papa waddled behind. Meeting up behind the hill, Klaarongah helped Krawwgh get out of his costume while Klengah watched in a child-like trance. Afterwards, Klaarongah sprinted off with Klengah at her side.

Krawwgh watched them with loving pride, as they tore off across the flat and arid plains, in search of prey. Both Klaarongah and Krawwgh were thrilled and greatly relieved, when Nbegwe told them about Klengah's brave encounter with the deadly cobra that had slithered into the camp one night, and how easily she had dispensed with the creature. This eased their worries about Klengah's survival on her own. Krawwgh drifted into a well-earned snooze and dreamed about his daughter and her brave encounter with the snake. Two hours later, Klaarongah and Klengah returned with a big, boar warthog, that Klengah had chased down and killed. Once again, mother and father beamed with pride, as they watched their little chick stab, chomp, and swallow big chunks of the delicious pig, before joining in. Afterwards, they peacefully squatted at the base of the big hill, grousing up and swallowing small stones to aid their digestion while cuddled together for warmth and affection, with Klengah nestled between them. Krawwgh and Klaarongah stared up at the black, starry night sky while their daughter slumbered peacefully from her exhausting big day.

They all arose at dawn and yawned and stretched themselves awake. Klaarongah took Klengah by the hand, and they trotted into the distance to relieve themselves, while Krawwgh spied on the ostriches. They had moved a few yards further away but remained intact with the same members as yesterday. Krawwgh donned his ostrich costume again and resumed his duties. This time, his battle with the alpha male was even shorter. Apparently, the bird still had some stinging memories from their encounter, yesterday. Again, Krawwgh's victory was noticed by the females, and his artificial courting rituals induced the desired effects. He spent more time with the females than ever before, as he took cloacal-canal readings and implanted more tracking devices, along with delivering his engineered semen. He wanted to keep the females as aroused and interested as possible, so he periodically gave chase to the subordinate males to impress and bond the females to himself only, hoping that this heightened state might increase the chance of conception.

As Krawwgh was finishing up with one of the females, Klengah bounded out among the flock again, but displayed a quieter, more demure approach. She joined a group of females and juveniles busy grousing for worms and beetles. She hadn't been at the task long before that same male noticed her again, and began his mating behavior repertoire. Klaarongah was hiding behind the hill, watching and hoping for a link-up, but was ready to intercede in case of violence. Perhaps, reassured by being surrounded by the other big females and juveniles, Klengah joined the other females when they assumed their squats and didn't resist the male this time when he came up behind her. Klaarongah and Krawwgh were ecstatic when they realized their daughter was enjoying the new but natural sensation! This filled them both with great relief, not because of any anticipated pregnancy, but rather because their very social daughter would at least be able to enjoy the pleasures of sex! As a hybrid creature, her chances of ever conceiving were quite low indeed. As it turned out, that couple of days they spent together were quite special and productive. Krawwgh had successfully completed his best efforts yet in trans-species fertilizations, while both of the loving and worried parents saw that their daughter was able to adjust, live, and thrive in her world.

They returned to their tribe the next day, and neither Klaarongah nor Krawwgh could wait to brag to anyone nearby about the exploits of their daring young daughter and how much she had matured. Nbegwe and the elders were truly delighted, and they all crowded around to hug her. For her part, Klengah basked in all the loving attention again, as she would for many years to come. As with any lives, many low times accompanied the highs, as Klengah and many of her tribe grew up, while Klaarongah, Krawwgh, and the tribal elders grew old and eventually died. Old Mntangua was first. He died from natural causes after living an honest and noble life within the tribe he loved, and with his best friend Klengah at his side. Despite his continued efforts through many ostrich breeding seasons, Krawwgh never once was successful in impregnating any of the ostriches. The myriad challenges posed by trying to engineer compatible gene locations on artificial protein scaffoldings, coupled with his advancing age and its concomitant reduction in viable sperm cells, eventually spelled the end for this part of their otherwise highly successful mission to Earth. There would be no permanent establishment of beings bearing the many noble traits and mental abilities of their doomed race. Klengah was the youngest of their kind and soon to be the only one left.

One hot spring that fateful day came. Now, Klengah was a middle-age adult even though she was still stuck in a childhood, mentally. She hugged her frail and elderly parents goodbye. Then, did the same to Nbegwe's daughter, Ndula, who had recently been elected the tribe's new leader and physician, after the natural passing of her very old mother. Klengah was leaving the tribe to spend a couple of days with her other friends, the ostriches, where she could relax with beings much more like herself physically, and enjoy some sexual release. The timing was perfect because neither Krawwgh nor Klaarongah could physically play and engage their loving daughter anymore, and they didn't want to put her through the terrible anguish and worrisome confusion she'd surely suffer, watching their continued deterioration and death. Krawwgh's mighty wings had finally seized with a severely crippling arthritis, and Klaarongah was rapidly wasting away, because she could no longer eat. Their loving tribe members willingly shared anything they had with them, but since Klaarongah and Krawwgh had taught them all they would need to live and thrive long into the future and Klengah could be spared the trauma of a permanent goodbye, Klaarongah and Krawwgh decided to act now.

As soon as Klengah had disappeared into the distant plains, Krawwgh asked Ndula to please gather up all available tribe members. Through their helmets, which were set on maximum audible interpretation, they began to slowly and painfully dance-announce their intentions and offer their profound thanks and love to all. They would soon board their ship and leave them forever. Many were crying and wailing upon hearing the news, but most of them completely understood, and all of them would comply with their wishes and plans. They deserved no less from people they had loved so completely, and for so long!

Starting with Ndula and the tribal council of elders, the huge crowd approached and they offered their parting hugs and kisses goodbye to the both of them. When all of the tribe had said their farewells, Krawwgh asked his last favor of them, to wander off a good distance so as to remain safe from the life pod's enormous blast upon takeoff. They didn't have to ask the tribe to look after Klengah, or to soothe her fears and sorrows upon discovering their permanent absence, because they knew everyone loved her as their own. SHE WAS TRIBE! They also had complete confidence in these new humans and how good they would be from now on. Klaarongah and Krawwgh had done all they could for them and could now rest easy as they faced the inevitable.

When they judged the tribe was at a safe distance, Klaarongah inserted the launch sequence codes, and they both assumed their positions on the safety hammocks and belted in. Then, the pilot helmets descended from the ceiling ports and settled on their heads. Now, they were reconnected to the life pod's computer neural network again and able to oversee and override—if necessary—the automatic pilot and flight control. 60-some years had passed since the vessel had last flown, but telemetry was pouring in from all over the huge ship, indicating that everything was nominal and all systems were go. First, a faint hissing indicated that the nuclear fusion reactor was filling with its fusion fuel mix of hydrogen and deuterium with a neutron catalyst mix of lithium fumes. Then, several pulsing magnets switched on to begin squeezing the fuel mixture toward it's critical density, while lasers and neutrons were pulsed into the reactor chamber to further heat up and crush the plasma. At this point, the plasma compound was instantly crushed under the pressure of billions of times that of the air outside, while simultaneously heating up to over 100 million degrees, causing a blast of glaring red, ionized hydrogen exhaust gas to exit the engine nozzles and lift the vessel skyward.

Over a mile away, the tribe was stunned by the sound of the blast and then the roaring-red glare as the huge vessel hurtled up into the sky and away into space. Since they hadn't been told where it was bound, they could only speculate and wish their dear teachers and friends a safe and glorious final journey among the stars. What none of them knew was that Klaarongah and Krawwgh had an absolute obligation to once again, assure, that such a powerful and capable vessel never ended up in wrong hands, somehow. Its fate would parallel that of the drones. After a leisure flyby of the planets, Venus and Mercury, their ship would automatically pilot itself to crash into the sun. If both or either of them still had the strength left, they could view and enjoy the vistas each planet offered. If not, it wouldn't matter as they would be lovingly bonded to face their end together, at one another's side.

Several days later—back on Earth—a tired and happy Klengah bounded into the camp and into the awaiting arms of Ndula and the tribe. She couldn't tell them how happy she was and how much fun she had running, chasing, and mating with her fellow bird-beings, nor could she communicate how much she had missed them all while she was away. Just then, Ndula's twin little boys ran into the hut and jumped up on Klengah to smother her in hugs and kisses. She gently squeezed them both in her big forelimbs and gave them both an eye-kiss, just like her mama and papa always did to her. That memory immediately distracted her from the joy of the children, and she gently set them down to go after her parents. Ndula followed behind, with her boys in tow. At first, she let out some gentle caws and squawks but heard nothing in return. She became fearful, and started honking and squawking even louder. Still nothing, so she trotted over to where their big 'house' was, and began panicking when she couldn't find it. With tears welling up in her beautiful eyes, Ndula reached out and called for Klengah.

Klengah returned to her and gave her wet eyes a kiss with one of her own big ones, but then gently tugged on Ndula's arm, directing her to come and help find her parents. Scooping up both of her little boys, Ndula followed Klengah as fast as she safely could, over to the scorched greenish glass that had resulted from the life pod's departure. Ndula reached out again and gently stroked Klengah's arm while trying to distract her from her terrible state. Klengah felt the greenish glass crumple under her huge talons but could not find that house where Mama and Papa stayed. Then, pathetically, Klengah started cawing and honking again, trying desperately to contact her folks. She started running in circles around the launch site. All Ndula could do was watch her and cry while the incredibly sad display continued to unfold. Whenever Klengah would pause from the frantic chase, Ndula would try to smile and point skyward, hoping that somehow she would begin to understand. This went on for several minutes, and finally, the little boys grew tired and cold and began to whimper.

Ndula made a walking gesture, indicating that she was going back to her tent and wanted Klengah to join them. Klengah wouldn't or couldn't. She had to find her parents. Ndula turned and walked slowly back to camp, weeping and wondering whether Klaarongah or Krawwgh knew how upset and inconsolable their daughter would become upon discovering their permanent disappearance. The next morning, Ndula awoke to see her toddlers still dreamily snoozing, but no signs of Klengah. She ran over to her younger sister's hut and rapped on the wood post. Mnaiya awoke and covered herself in her tunic, as Ndula briefed her about last night and asked her to look after her boys. Mnaiya yawned and nodded yes, then followed Ndula back to her hut with her dozing sons. Ndula reached into the covered lime-pit and retrieved a large dry fish to lure Klengah back to the hut. Then, she trotted out to last night's location. Only a few minutes later, she was there and was startled by what she saw. Klengah was asleep but still fidgeting, and her talons were bleeding—no doubt from the big circular rut she had created from her panicked and pathetic exertions all night. It appeared she had plucked out some of her belly feathers in some sad fit as well. The scent of the fish soon caused her to stir, and Ndula gently stroked her head and neck plumage as she placed the fish underneath her big bill. This aroused her, but instead of devouring the fish, Klengah jumped up and began her panicked pacing around the circle again, while loudly squawking and honking for her parents.

This went on for the rest of the day and into the night as she ceaselessly continued to squawk, honk, caw, and pace around the circular rut, never stopping to eat or drink. Whenever they could break from their children and chores, Ndula, Mnaiya, and others would try to soothe Klengah and get her to drink and eat, but they all failed, and at the end of the third day, they were at wit's end and beginning to panic themselves. They were truly afraid that if she kept this up for much longer, she would kill herself, and none of them could bear the thought. It was then that one of the hunters volunteered the idea of blow-darting her with a powerful anesthetic. Of course, this meant scaling down a really big dose of one of their poisons, and made for a lot of guess work on just how much they should use. Too little, and it would likely add to her hysteria and might make her very dangerous; too much and it could kill her, their beloved special charge and fellow tribe member. One thing was certain, the situation had to change pretty soon. Anything was better than watching her destroy herself this way.

With all the love and care they could muster, Ndula, Mnaiya, and some of the rest of the tribe took their turns trying desperately to calm and soothe poor Klengah, and as the night closed in, the hunters began planning for the darting at dawn.

Before daybreak the next morning, Klengah finally gave in and swallowed the pungent fish. It was an ecstatic relief for the huge bird. She had lost nearly 40 pounds in three days. Not only did it calm her tremendous hunger, but it seemed to quell her panic as well. She couldn't understand what had happened to her mama and papa, and she would always wonder where they were, but she did know where Ndula and her tribe were, and she was NEVER going to lose them! She wearily trotted on her very sore talons down that path that she knew so very well, and quietly ducked into Ndula's tent. Just as exhausted from loving, worry, and sadness as she was, Ndula was sound asleep and didn't hear Klengah come in, but she stirred a bit as she felt her bed shake from 400 pounds of giant bird flopping next to her, and then felt her head rest gently on top of her turned shoulder.

Ndula's beautiful brown eyes sprung open, and she turned to face her bewildered and traumatized SISTER. She sobbed tears of joy and kissed and hugged Klengah tightly, absolutely overjoyed that she had come back to them on her own volition and that somehow her love had reached her through her tragic grief and destructive despair. Together, they slept soundly cuddled in each other's arms, and before they finally stirred awake late the next morning, the whole tribe was in a hushed, ecstatic buzz and relieved by the adorable scene of the two exhausted 'sisters' still embracing in deep sleep, with a toddler boy dozing on each of Klengah's feathery flanks. Unknown to them all, however—even to the mightiest and most intelligent beings that had ever sprinted across Earth's plains or hurtled from its skies—there was someone else peacefully snoozing. Deep inside Klengah's mighty body was someone yet to let its presence be known. Klengah, the unlikely to ever conceive hybrid, WAS PREGNANT. And with a little luck and lots of help from her loving tribe, she, too, would eventually become an attentive and adoring middle-aged mama to some future 'darling of the camp.'